G

FRIENDS
OF ACPL

W9-CZX-097

THE DEVIL'S HORSE

TALES FROM THE KALEVALA

by Keith Bosley

PANTHEON

FOR BENJAMIN

CONTENTS

Introduction   ix

The Beginning   3

Singing Match   8

Aino   17

Iron   27

The Sampo   41

The Devil's Horse   50

Väinämöinen   69

The Wedding   82

The Expedition   103

The Battle   114

Moon, Sun and Fire   126

Mighty Music   142

INTRODUCTION

"One man, by running around, has set things to rights for us." These words, borrowed from a writer of ancient Rome, are printed under a cartoon which appeared in Finland in 1847. The cartoon shows a man hurrying barefoot across open country. He is carrying a rucksack; in his right hand is a walking stick, and in his left hand is a scroll of paper.

His name is Elias Lönnrot. He is a doctor whose work often takes him into the remote country districts of Finland. When he has treated his patients, he listens to their ballads and songs. There are tales of great deeds long ago, love songs, spells to bring a good harvest, and spells—of particular interest to him—for healing wounds and diseases. For some years now he has been collecting these songs and publishing them, along with articles about them and the people who sing them. They often sing to the accompaniment of the *kantele*, a kind of small harp which they hold across their knees and pluck. Lönnrot's collection of such songs is called *Kanteletar*, a word which means something like "the spirit-daughter of the *kantele*." Lönnrot's other great collection, on which the present book is based, is called *Kalevala*, which some people take to mean "the land of heroes." Published in two installments, in 1835 and 1849, the *Kalevala* consists of several groups of heroic ballads arranged to form a narrative poem of some 23,000 lines, the "national epic" of Finland.

If you look at a map of Europe, you will see that Finland lies, as someone has said, "between east and west, and a little to the north." On both sides this country of only four and a half million people has neighbors bigger and stronger than herself—to the east, Russia, and to the west, Sweden. For centuries Finland was a part of Sweden, and all the important people in Finland spoke Swedish. Finnish was the language of country folk, and little attention was paid to it or to them until Lönnrot published the ballads and songs he had collected. Here was proof that Finland had a character of her own, a heritage to be proud of. The Finns started taking an interest in themselves as Finns: poets and playwrights and novelists began to write in Finnish rather than Swedish, painters turned to the *Kalevala* for inspiration, composers—of whom the greatest was Sibelius— set out to write music which would be unmistakably Finnish. Since those days Finland has become an independent nation, and although the Soviet Union bit off a large chunk of her eastern provinces during the Second World War, an independent nation she remains to this day. And largely because of a country doctor and his folklore; hence that cartoon which said: "One man, by running around, has set things to rights for us."

It was not only the Finns who took the *Kalevala* to their hearts. The poem was translated into several languages. A German version found its way to the United States, where Henry Wadsworth Longfellow read it.

He was so excited that he produced an imitation of it, using the same metre to describe the adventures of an imaginary Indian hero; this was *The Song of Hiawatha*. The present book brings you nearly all the *Kalevala* stories. If you would like to go on from here, you could read the whole poem in the verse translation by W. F. Kirby, published by Dutton, or in the more recent prose translation by Francis Peabody Magoon, Jr., published by the Harvard University Press.

A word now about proper names. These are often long and rather difficult at first, but you will soon get used to them. The basic rule is to pronounce every letter —there are no confusing silent letters as there are in English. Double letters sound like single ones, only longer. Letters to remember particularly are:

- a: almost like *u* in *hut*
- h: always sounded, even after a vowel
- j: like *y* in *yes*
- u: as in *put*
- ä: like *a* in *hat*
- ö: like *eu* in French *deux*; shape your tongue to sound *e*, and your lips to sound *o*

Always stress the first vowel in a word: for example *POhjola, MArjatta, VÄinämöinen, LUonnotar.*

Finnish is an ancient and beautiful language with many unfamiliar sounds, but we do not need to know them for this book.

THE DEVIL'S HORSE

TALES FROM THE KALEVALA

THE BEGINNING

As they sat by their stoves during the long winter evenings, the Finns of old used to wonder; how did it all begin—these long lakes, these great green forests covered with snow? And ourselves, how did we begin?

And they imagined that the world had had a mother. This mother they called at first the Maid of the Air, and her first child, they imagined, was the Water—all the lakes and rivers and seas of the world.

Tired of floating in the Air, this Mother came down and lay in the Water she had produced, and so was called the Water Mother.

Now a huge Bird came flying over the Water, looking for somewhere to lay her eggs; but, of course, there was no dry land yet. Then what should the Bird see but the Water Mother; and the Water Mother, seeing the Bird, lifted one of her knees up out of the Water for the Bird to rest on.

The Bird came wheeling down and settled on the knee. Before the Water Mother knew what was happening, the Bird had laid her eggs on her knee and was sitting on them to hatch them out.

For a long, long time the Bird sat on her eggs, which grew warmer and warmer. So, the knee on which she sat grew warmer as well. Hotter and hotter it grew . . .

3

until the Water Mother could bear the heat no longer, and she drew her knee back into the cool water.

The Bird, no doubt, was furious. And what happened to the eggs? Well, they were smashed to pieces. But never mind; it was just as well they did break, for the bottom halves of the shells became the earth and the top halves became the sky. The yolks of the eggs became the sun and the whites became the moon. The speckled parts of the shells became the stars, and the dark parts became the clouds.

Then, said the Finns of old, the Water Mother made all the other things in the world, until at last she gave birth to a human child; but Väinämöinen, her son, had waited so long to be born that he had grown quite old, and had a long white beard.

After tossing about in the Water for some time, Väinämöinen reached land. Being a good Finn, he needed to have forests around him before he could be happy. He found a little man who had been born of the earth, who sowed some seeds for him.

Up sprang trees, among them an oak so immense that its leaves shut out the sun and moon; and the whole world was in darkness.

"What is to happen now?" Väinämöinen asked himself, stroking his beard. "The whole world is in darkness and all mankind will live in sorrow. O Luonnotar, Mother Nature, surely there is a creature in the waters strong and powerful enough to fell this great oak for me."

At that moment there was a swirling of the waters, and out of them rose—not a monster, nor a mighty beast, nor even a giant fish—but a tiny man no bigger than Väinämöinen's thumb. Fully armed for battle he was, with a copper helmet, copper boots, with gloves of copper on his tiny hands. Around his waist was a shining copper belt in which was tucked a bright copper axe, its blade no bigger than a fingernail.

"A fine fellow you look," said Väinämöinen to him, "in your gallant outfit. But you are hardly the man to fell this towering oak!" And he chuckled into his beard at the thought of the little man hacking at the tree, himself no bigger than an acorn.

"Small I may be," replied the copper-clad figure with its shrill little voice, "but I have come to remove that oak for you." And he waved his axe calmly at the oak as though it were a blade of grass.

As Väinämöinen watched, unable to believe his eyes, the man grew, and grew, and grew, until his head disappeared into the clouds. Then he stooped to sharpen his axe—which had grown with him—and started work.

The axe swung into the tree's trunk—once, twice, and at the third stroke there was a shudder and a creak, and down thundered the oak with a terrible crash.

The sun came out once more, now that the shadow of the oak was gone. The other trees put on their leaves, the birds sang in the warm light. Everything grew and flourished from that moment onward—everything, except the Barley.

Now, Barley is made into beer, and Väinämöinen could not imagine life without good, wholesome barley beer to drink. But Barley simply refused to grow. Väinämöinen walked down by the water's edge, wondering what to do, when on the sand he found a barleycorn. With great joy he picked it up and told himself, "Barley needs room to grow. I must have a wide field of Barley if there is to be enough beer for the whole world to drink."

And because the man from the water had vanished, he set bravely to felling the other trees himself.

After much swinging of his axe, the land was clear of trees and ready for the planting of the barleycorn. One tree, however, he spared; one graceful silver birch, shimmering in the sunlight.

"Why have you left the birch tree standing?" asked a deep voice from the air. It was the eagle, king of the birds.

"Your Majesty," replied Väinämöinen politely, "I have left the birch tree standing so that your subjects have somewhere to roost in this treeless land."

"How very kind," boomed the eagle, hovering above his head. "As a sign of my gratitude, O wise man, here is some fire to burn the trees you have felled."

Down flew a spark which began eating the trees which were lying all around. Soon the fire was roaring merrily and the trees were so many heaps of ash. The ash was good for the soil, making it rich and fertile.

6

Väinämöinen sowed his barleycorn and called to Ukko, the Old Man, Lord of the Weather, to look after it and bring it up well with plenty of sunshine to cheer it, and plenty of rain to nourish it.

Scarcely a week had gone by when the land was covered with whispering, waving barley as far as the eye could see. Väinämöinen was happy at last.

"Why have you left the birch tree standing?" asked another voice from the air. This time it was the cuckoo. Now the cuckoo loves the warm weather and Finland has only a short summer; so when the cuckoo comes all the way to Finland, skies are going to be blue for some time.

"I have left the birch tree standing so that you and your kind have somewhere to roost," replied Väinämöinen. "Welcome, O cuckoo. Please stay with us, that our fair land may echo with your call."

SINGING MATCH

ow that he had sown his barley, Väinämöinen could rest awhile with his thoughts, and, no doubt, his *kantele* as well; for he sang. Day and night he sang his wondrous songs. By now there were other people on the earth, and they would stop to listen; but nobody really understood the songs. They were clearly songs of great age and wisdom, but their meaning was too profound for any but the oldest and wisest of men. In fact, they were also songs of power, and their singer could make them work for him, as we shall see before very long.

News of Väinämöinen's singing spread across the countryside, across the meadows, sweet in the morning sunlight, over the shining lakes, through the dark forests and beyond the gloomy heathlands spread the fame of the wise old man, like seeds on the wind. All the way to the North Land people talked of Väinämöinen.

Pohjola, the North Land, was a cold, silent place where it was nearly always winter. Some folk say that the North Land of the Tales is the country we know as Lapland, where the sun rises at the beginning of the short summer, shines day and night a few weeks, then sets, leaving the land in dusk and darkness for the rest of the year. Other folk say it is in central Finland, along the west coast between the modern towns of Oulu and

Vaasa; but wherever it was, the North Land was not such a pleasant place as Kalevala.

There was a young man of the North Land whose name was Joukahainen. A handsome fellow he was, with black hair and quick, dark eyes—quite different to look at from the fair-haired men of the south. He fancied himself as a singer of songs, and was generally rather conceited. When he heard about Väinämöinen's songs of wisdom, he frowned.

"Who is this old man people call a greater singer than I?" he scowled.

He called to his mother. "Mother," he said, "I'm going on a long journey. I'm going south to meet this old Väinämöinen, who is supposed to sing such marvelous songs."

His father overheard him and said, "Don't be so foolish, my son. Being so old Väinämöinen is bound to be wiser than you. Why, you're little more than a boy still!"

"No, don't go, son," his mother pleaded. "The songs of the great Väinämöinen will surely bring you to harm, if you don't respect them."

His beautiful sister Aino said nothing, but the almost frightened look in her dark eyes showed that she would rather he stayed at home.

"Your advice, Father," Joukahainen declared, "is sound; and yours, dear Mother, is even better; but my own, the advice I give myself, is best of all. I shall go today and challenge the old fool to a singing match. What could be fairer than that? And who knows, *my* songs may well bring *him* to harm—if he doesn't trip over his beard first!"

Without another word he strapped on his sword, took his crossbow and arrows, called his dog, then went to the stable and got out his horse. In no time at all he had harnessed it to his sledge and was dashing off across the gleaming snow, leaving parents and sister looking after him, shaking their heads sadly.

For three days he rode southwards over the white land, forests rushing by to his right, lakes to his left, till on the third day he saw grass and flowers and knew he was in Kalevala, the fair home of Väinämöinen.

Who was that on the road just ahead of him? It was an old man—for he could see white hair and a flowing white beard—driving his sledge peacefully along. He must be admiring the scenery, for he was moving quite slowly.

Joukahainen had no time for old men, scenery or anything that got in his way. He drove a little faster until he came level with the old man, and as he passed pushed him over to the side of the road.

"Hey, watch where you're going!" cried the old man as Joukahainen forced him to a stop. "You've damaged my sledge with your clumsiness—look, the runners are all splintered! Who do you think you are, careering along without a care for anyone else?"

"I," said the young man with great importance, "am Joukahainen. And who, may I ask, are you?"

But the old man only said, "If you are Joukahainen, you must move aside for me. After all, you are the younger."

"Ha!" said Joukahainen scornfully. "Difference of age is no concern of mine. Why, I know who you are, old man; you are Väinämöinen, the great, the wise singer. Come now, let us sing together, to see who is the better singer. I'm sure," he added with a smirk, "that we have much to learn from one another."

"Tell me, then," said Väinämöinen, "what can you sing about."

"Oh, many things," answered the young man airily, waving a gloved hand. "I will give you some examples. My wisdom has taught me that the smoke-hole is in the roof, and the fire in the hearth. Furthermore, fish like to swim. Shall I go on?"

Väinämöinen said nothing.

"Very well," said Joukahainen. "Now, in the north the plough is drawn by reindeer, while in the south it is drawn by horses. I know many mountains, and I am well acquainted with lakes and waterfalls."

"All this is common knowledge," said Väinämöinen, shrugging his shoulders, "but I suppose it is quite good for a start. Now tell me things of real wisdom you can sing about, tell me now of great matters, such as only the wisest understand."

"With pleasure," said Joukahainen. "Let me see. Ah, yes; I am an expert on birds, snakes and fish. Iron is hard. Black mud is bitter to the tongue. Boiling water is painful, and so is fire.

"I am very good at history too," he went on. "For instance, did you know, old man, that the first houses in this land were built of wood, and the first pots made of stone?"

Väinämöinen was speechless. Here was a boy, telling him, the first man on earth, things he not only knew, but had seen with his own eyes long ago.

"Is that," said Väinämöinen, trying not to lose his temper, "is that the end of your nonsense?"

"Oh no," said Joukahainen brightly, "nor is it nonsense. Only silly old men would call it nonsense." Even so, he was a little uneasy by now, and he began to boast.

"It was I who ploughed the sea bed and dug out the caves where the fish live," he claimed. "It was I who filled the lakes with water and heaped up the mountains. It was I who fixed the pillars the sky rests on. It was I who set the sun and moon on their courses, and hung the stars in the winter sky. It was I who . . ."

"What a shameless liar you are!" howled Väinämöinen in a rage. "What do you know, you puppy, about how it all began? Why, when I cleared the forests and planted barley you were not so much as a speck of dust. How dare you waste my time with such —such talk!"

"So I am a liar?" shouted Joukahainen, his eyes ablaze. "All right, then, and if I am, what are you going to do about it?"

He drew his sword and brandished it at the old man. "Draw your sword, grandad, if it isn't too heavy for you to hold, and we'll soon see who is the better man!"

"I wouldn't take the trouble," replied Väinämöinen without moving. "Draw my sword on you? Why," he laughed, "a slip of a lad like you wouldn't stand a chance!"

"An old coward as well as an old fool, I see!" the young man blustered. "Very well," he said, putting his sword back in its sheath. "I'll just sing one of my songs and you will turn into a pig. I can, you know. There's many a pig in the North Land that was once somebody who upset me!"

We shall never know whether Joukahainen could sing such a powerful song, for at that moment Väinämöinen could stand no more, and began to sing himself.

He sang a song such as only the oldest and wisest can sing. It was a song of great matters, a song of life and of death. As he sang, the lakes swelled up, the earth shook, and the mountains trembled like silver birch trees in autumn. Joukahainen trembled too as he saw the runners of his sledge turn back into the saplings they were made of. The wooden collar his horse was wearing turned into a willow tree, and the reins became an alder tree. Then the sledge itself rose into the air, floated out over a lake not far from the road, and disappeared in the water. His whip, which was lying on the ground at his feet, became a reed at the lake's edge, and his horse—without so much as a neigh it turned into a stone.

Joukahainen felt something slithering at his waist. It was his sword; it rose out of its sheath, streaked high into the air and became a flash of lightning. On his back his crossbow twitched, and taking his arrows with it flew up into the air as well, where it turned into a rainbow and the arrows into a flock of birds. And his dog, without so much as a whimper, turned into another stone along with his horse.

For the first time in his life Joukahainen was terrified. He just stood there helpless as Väinämöinen sang on and on.

Puff! Off came his hat, and there was a cloud in the sky he had not noticed before. And over there, on the lake, what strange looking water-lilies? Then he realized he had lost his gloves . . . Off flew his coat too, another cloud. And the belt with the shining studs he was so proud of, away it squirmed and the studs became so many stars, which, because it was daytime, vanished in the blue sky.

Still Väinämöinen sang, and—horror!—Joukahainen felt himself moving. Suddenly splash he went into the black mud at the lakeside. It was deep, sticky mud, and Joukahainen started sinking. Down he sank, and, struggle as he might, he could not stop himself.

"Old man, dear, wise old man," he called out to Väinämöinen, "sing another song to save me from this mud, and I will give you whatever you ask!"

"And what," replied Väinämöinen, "do you imagine you have that I could possibly want?"

"I have two crossbows which never miss their mark," called the young man. "You may choose either of them!"

"I have crossbows in plenty," said Väinämöinen, and continued singing. Down went Joukahainen another inch or so in the mud.

"I have two boats, one good for racing, the other good for carrying heavy loads," he called. "Have which one you like!"

"I am well provided with boats," said Väinämöinen. "All my creeks are full of them, waiting to be used." And he went on singing. Down went Joukahainen a few more inches.

"I have two fine horses, one good for bearing news, the other good for pulling the plough," he called. "Either of them is yours!"

"Horses, did you say?" said Väinämöinen. "I have stables full of them." And he took up his song once more. Joukahainen grew desperate. He offered a fine helmet, any amount of gold and silver, his crops, his fields, everything he possessed and probably a good deal besides; but Väinämöinen, it seemed, had everything he wanted. Then Joukahainen had an idea.

"O wisest of singers," he called, "if you will save me I will give you my . . . my beautiful sister Aino, the Peerless One, to be your wife!"

Väinämöinen stopped singing. You could have heard a birch leaf fall. Yes, he had everything he wanted, but indeed who was there to share it with, who was there to care for him in his old age?

He began singing again—but it was a different song this time. Joukahainen squelched upward out of the mud, and before he knew where he was, he was back on dry land standing before Väinämöinen, who was singing more sweetly than he had ever sung before.

Joukahainen's coat descended softly on to his shoulders. Around his waist slipped his belt. His hat flew down and settled on his head. His gloves slid back on his hands. Crossbow and arrows returned; so did his sledge, complete with runners. There was his dog—and his horse, wearing collar and reins; and here was his whip.

Without a word he leaped on his sledge, gave the horse a touch of the whip, and galloped off northward leaving a great shower of snow behind him.

AINO

It was a deeply troubled Joukahainen who returned home to the North Land. He loved his sister Aino dearly, and now thanks to him she was to spend the rest of her life looking after an old man.

His mother asked him what the matter was. It was so unlike her Joukahainen, she thought, to be walking about with downcast eyes. He told her that Väinämöinen had put a spell on him—which was more or less true—with the result he had promised Aino to him as his wife. He did not understand why his mother laughed and clapped her hands.

"This is no time for sadness, my son," she said gaily. "Väinämöinen, the great, wise Väinämöinen to be my son-in-law! What an honor to our family! How people will look up to us! Spell or no spell, you're a very clever boy and I'm proud of you!" And she went to embrace him, but Joukahainen walked away.

The dreadful thing about it all was, of course, that nobody had asked Aino how she felt. She was sitting quietly by the fire, sewing as usual, her long dark hair with its bright ribbons falling across her shoulders. Suddenly the needle slipped from her fingers and she burst into sobs.

"Aino, darling! Don't cry, little one," said her mother, going over to her. "You are to have the finest husband of them all. Just think how people will point to you and whisper, 'Aino? Yes, she is the wife of the great Väinämoinen; of all the most beautiful girls in the world he chose her.' "

"But, Mother," Aino sobbed, "I don't want to marry yet. I don't want to leave everybody and everything here at home—not for a long time yet."

"Oh, but you'll have a loving husband, and a far grander house than ours, and you'll make lots of interesting new friends," said her mother. "How I wish I were a young girl again, with a chance like this!"

People! All her mother was thinking about was people—how they would look up to her. Aino did not want to be looked up to. She was not a difficult girl; all she wanted in life was one day to marry a pleasant young man who would love her and care for her—not a touchy old fellow, however famous he was, who expected to be waited on hand and foot and would probably give nothing in return. But there it was; she had never had an argument with her mother, and she was not sure how to go about one. Besides, her mother had never been like this before. With a heavy heart she got up from her seat by the fire and went out for a walk, wondering what to do.

She had not walked very far when she heard a rustling in some bushes nearby. Being a country girl she was not afraid—it was probably a bird. But it was a man, in fact it was Väinämöinen himself. He had come all the way to the North Land to see this girl he was to marry. She was so beautiful, with her long hair and dark eyes, that he recognized her at once. It could only be Aino.

"Young lady," he said rather quaintly, going up to her, "for me wear that lovely necklace of yours, and for me tie those ribbons in your hair!"

Aino recognized the old man too. She had heard of those twinkling eyes, that long white beard.

"No I will not!" she answered him, her voice sharp with the fright he had given her. "I will wear whatever I like, to please myself and nobody else! And I am quite happy living at home with my family, thank you very much!"

She tore the hateful ribbons out of her hair and pulled off her necklace and flung them on the ground at Väinämöinen's feet. Then, not knowing what to do next, she turned and ran all the way home.

"What is it? What's the matter?" cried her mother and father and brother when she came dashing in, with tears running down her cheeks.

"Oh," she wept, "I have lost my ribbons and the necklace I loved so much!"

Her mother did not believe her and she took her aside.

"Now, my girl," she said kindly, "you can tell your mother the real cause of your trouble. Come along."

"Väinämöinen," gulped Aino, "he's here. I saw him. He asked me to wear my necklace and the ribbons in my hair to please him, so I took them off and threw them on the ground, just to show him."

"Dear me, dear me," her mother smiled, drying her tears, "and is that all? There now. Don't you think it was rather rude of you to treat your future husband in this way?"

Aino was just about to protest when her mother went on, "And you're not looking your best, either. Plenty of butter for you, young woman, and plenty of cream cakes. That'll put a bloom on your cheeks and fill you out a bit. He won't want you if you're pale and skinny!"

Aino was horrified. What had happened to the mother she knew and loved so well? She was quite possessed with the idea of her marrying this aged man; it was almost as though he had put a spell on her too. And still she talked, getting more and more excited.

"Go to the mountain—the one with the secret cave I told you of when you were a little girl. There you will find some boxes and chests. Open them and you will find six golden girdles and seven finely woven blue gowns. These were made by the daughters of the sun and the moon for me, when I was going to marry your father. I've kept them all these years to give you when you marry. Go and fetch them—quickly now!"

Aino found her tongue at last.

"Oh, Mother, Mother," she said, "what has happened? Can't you see I don't want to marry Väinämöinen? When I marry it will be to a young man, not an old man who trips over his stockings."

But her mother's mind was made up, and off went

poor Aino along the road that led to the mountain with the secret cave. As she passed the lakes she thought how she was once as happy as water sparkling and dancing in the sun; now, it seemed, she was like water in a deep well. As she passed through the dim forests, she thought how her once joyful heart was now like the dead, tangled bushes whose thorns were tearing at her skirt.

Here at last was the mountain, and—look—here was the cave. It was so dark and still inside that she felt she must go on tiptoe. Yes, there were the boxes and the chests. She went over and pulled at the lid of the biggest one. It opened with a creak that made her jump. She lifted the clothes out, blew the dust off them, and took them to the mouth of the cave to look at them in the sunlight.

Six golden girdles! She went back and opened another chest.

Seven finely woven blue gowns! Truly, she thought, these had been made by the daughters of the sun and the moon!

She could not resist trying on one of the seven gowns —the bluest of them all, blue as the summer sky. Perhaps it was a little too big for her, but after all she had not expected to wear it so soon in her life.

And now for one of the six girdles, how it glittered, like golden sunlight on a lake! She put it on and pulled the dress in around her slim waist.

In another chest Aino found . . . jewels! Gold and

silver buckles and hair pins; and here were ribbons by the dozen, sky blue and scarlet, to tie up her hair. In a very short time she was looking more beautiful than she had thought she could ever look. She walked around and around outside the cave, one minute holding her head high, the next looking back at the long dress trailing behind her.

Then she remembered. In her excitement she had nearly forgotten. She, Aino, was to be married to old Väinämöinen—and this was her wedding dress she had just put on!

For a moment she did not know what to do. Her mother's words rang in her ears in the silence, "Go and fetch them—quickly now!" Still wearing her wedding dress and the jewels and the ribbons in her hair, she ran out from under the mountain, but instead of going home she turned the other way.

Over the fields she ran, where the snow was melting at the approach of summer, past the swamps and the patches of wild heather, through the gloomy woodlands. On and on she ran, not knowing, not caring where she was going.

The sun was sinking now after the brief northern day and the quiet moon was rising over the tops of the tall trees. Just as she was feeling too tired to go any farther she saw a lake shining through the trees in front of her. It was like a long strip of silver laid across the black land. Oh, if only life could be as smooth and as peaceful as this lake! Indeed, it had been until now. She dropped exhausted to the ground and was soon asleep.

She was woken early the next morning by the birds calling to each other overhead. Aino wondered where she was at first, so deeply had she slept, but when she looked down at her blue dress—a little crumpled now—she remembered the day before and all its sorrow. She stood up, stretched herself and walked down to the lakeside. The waves looked so carefree as they glistened and rippled in the warm young sun. How she would love a bath, she thought, to wash away the shadows of the night, and the shadows of yesterday!

She untied the ribbons and took down the gold and silver buckles and hair pins out of her hair, so that it hung dark and soft and loose about her shoulders as it had always done. She took off the golden girdle and the sky-blue dress, and the rest of her clothes. She hung them all carefully on bushes and on the lower branches of trees, so as not to spoil them, and the jewels she laid on big flat stones, so as not to lose them. And she went down into the water.

It was still rather cold this fine morning in late spring, but the sun was beginning to take off the chill. She waded out a little way, feeling the sand and the small stones under her bare feet.

In the middle of the lake was a rock, just showing above the surface of the water. She swam slowly out toward it, enjoying the caress of the cool water around her body. She reached the rock and was clambering on to it when suddenly it sank beneath her. Perhaps she was tired after swimming so far, perhaps the water was still too cold for her, for she sank with the rock, and Aino, the Peerless One, was drowned.

Now, who will take the sad news home and break it to her family? Along lumbers a huge bear; he will go. But he has not gone far on his way when he sees a herd of cattle grazing in a meadow—and he forgets all about his errand. Then a wolf steals down to the lakeside; he will go. But he has not run many miles when he sees a flock of sheep—and he forgets too. Next comes a fox, carrying his bushy tail low; he will go. But he has hardly set out upon the journey when he hears his favorite delicacy cackling nearby—some fat, white geese. And when all the other animals have gone, up hops a hare with the longest ears in the North Land; he will go.

Away he skips, his white tuft of tail bobbing along behind him; he will not forget the message. Hopping and bobbing for hours on end he reaches the house where Aino lived.

"Ah, young scamp!" said her family when they spied him. "And what shall we do with you? Boil you for breakfast, or roast you for dinner?"

For once the hare was not afraid. He stuck his long ears straight up and said in his most important voice, "I ask you, what kind of meat runs to the pot to be cooked? I have a message; Aino, your Aino, is dead, drowned in a lake where she was bathing."

And suddenly he remembered he was a hare, and scampered off as fast as he could.

Everyone was heartbroken, but especially Aino's mother, who saw—now that it was too late—how cruel she had been, forcing her daughter to marry a man she did not love. She wept, and her tears flowed from her eyes down her cheeks. Down her cheeks they flowed, on to her breast. From her breast they flowed, and down her apron. Down her apron they flowed, on to the ground.

The tears ran along the ground and grew into streams; the streams swelled into three rivers, and the rivers thundered into three waterfalls. Out of the waterfalls rose three rocks, and upon the rocks sprang three silver birches, and in the crowns of the silver birches sat three golden cuckoos—those birds of good omen in a cold land.

One cuckoo called, "Sweetheart, sweetheart!" Another called, "Lover, lover!" And the third, "Gladness, gladness!"

The cuckoo who called "Sweetheart" sang to beautiful, dead Aino. The one who called "Lover" sang to Väinämöinen, a lonely old man. And the one who called "Gladness" sang to Aino's mother, whose tears would never stop flowing.

One day Väinämöinen was out fishing on the lake where Aino was drowned. He felt a tug on his net, and drew it up into his boat. There was a most marvelous fish—easily as big as a salmon. Even Väinämöinen could not help gazing at it as it lay panting at his feet.

"This fish," he said to himself, rubbing his hands together, "will be enough for both dinner and supper today—and tomorrow's breakfast too!"

He picked it up and was about to cut it open with his knife when it wriggled out of his hand and leaped over the side of the boat, back into the water. But instead of swimming away, the fish opened its mouth and spoke to the astonished old man.

"Even when I am a fish you cannot hold me!" it said. "I was Aino, the beautiful Aino whom you wanted for your wife."

And with a flick of its long tail the fish was gone, leaving only the waves of the lake sparkling and dancing in the sun.

IRON

Poor Väinämöinen was lonelier than ever. It was all very well being the oldest and wisest person in the land, but nobody really cared for him or even bothered with him; he was old enough and wise enough to look after himself! He must, he decided, find himself a wife.

One day Mother Nature, his mother, whispered to him in the noise of the waves, "Set out again, my son, for the North Land, and woo the Maid of the North. Go and woo the daughter of Louhi!"

Väinämöinen knew that Mother Nature usually gets her own way in the end, so without further ado he began the long journey northward—this time on horseback. And a marvelous horse it was; over the heathlands it galloped, through the forests, and when it came to a lake it even galloped across the water.

Unhappily things did not go smoothly for long—they were too good to be true, you might say. Väinämöinen was crossing a particularly long lake when his horse whinnied, faltered under him, and sank, plunging him into the water. A slight movement among the trees at the lakeside told him why.

Joukahainen, the young man who had caused so much sorrow, had heard from the noise of the waters that the old man was to pass this way; he had taken up his crossbow and his arrows and gone to wait for him. After seeing Väinämöinen fall into the lake he rode off, well content that he had had his revenge. But he had shot only Väinämöinen's horse, its rider was still very much alive, and swimming strongly on his way.

For many chilly days Väinämöinen struck out along the lake, while most men—even young men—would have swum to an island and wondered what to do. But now it was the turn of a friend to help out. There was a whirring of great wings in the sky, and a voice boomed: "Why, if it isn't my old friend Väinämöinen! And what brings you so far from home, swimming for all you're worth?"

Väinämöinen looked up. It was an eagle, that king of birds he had met when he was felling trees to plant his barley long ago. Väinämöinen told the eagle how he was on his way to the North Land to find a wife, and how he had had his horse shot from under him.

"I've been swimming for so many days," he concluded, "and there is still so far to go, that I don't know whether I shall die of hunger or drown first."

"Take heart, old friend," boomed the eagle. "Here, climb up on my back, and you shall fly the rest of your journey. I haven't forgotten the day you cleared the forests and spared the silver birch tree for my subjects to roost in. This is the least I can do in return for your consideration."

Väinämöinen climbed shivering out of the water on to the eagle's mighty shoulders. There was a rush of wing and wind, and before Väinämöinen could recover his wits the eagle had dropped him gently beside another lake—on the edge of the North Land. He opened his mouth to thank the eagle but all he saw was a black speck in the southern sky.

Wise Väinämöinen though he was, he felt quite lost and rather frightened, all alone in this bleak land with not a house in sight. There was only one word he could think of saying, and he said it.

"Help!" he called, and again, "Help! Does anybody live here?"

Silence—hardly an echo even; but far away somebody heard.

"Mother, I hear someone calling on the other side of the lake." It was the Maid of the North. She had just finished the housework with Louhi, her mother, and had gone out to empty her dustpan. "Whoever it is sounds as though he is in trouble."

Old Louhi, gap-toothed Mistress of the North, cupped her hand to her ear and listened too.

"Help! He—elp!" came the cry across the lake.

"That's no woman or child," said she. "That's the cry of a man—the moaning of a hero." And taking off her apron she hurried down to the lakeside where her boat was moored.

To his joy Väinämöinen saw a boat, rowed by an old woman, creaking and splashing through the waves toward him.

"Who are you, stranger?" called the old woman across the gloom, "and where do you come from?"

"I come from a fair country where my name is well known," Väinämöinen called back, feeling very sorry for himself. "But so much has happened to me on my way here, that I hardly know who I am any more!"

Louhi pulled in to the bank. The stranger had said enough for her to guess who he was. "Come home with me, Väinämöinen," she said kindly, helping him down into her boat and taking up the oars, "come and tell me your troubles."

At the farm on the other side of the lake he was treated with rare hospitality. He was washed with fine soap, rubbed with warm towels till he glowed, dressed in dry clothes, sat in front of a blazing fire, fed. When he felt himself again, Louhi asked him; "How come that you, the great Väinämöinen, were in such distress—so wet and cold, so lost?"

"Distress is the word," answered the old man mournfully. "I have been adrift in foreign waters. For days on end I swam the long lakes, not knowing what was to become of me. If only I had stayed at home, all this would not have happened."

"Poor Väinämöinen," said Louhi, patting his arm as though he were a small child, "you may stay here as long as you wish. There's salmon in the larder, and plenty of pork. I'm proud to have you as my guest."

"You're very kind," said Väinämöinen with a sad

smile, "but do you know, I'd rather be in my own country with my shoes letting in water, than live abroad and drink wine from cups of gold." He had clearly lost all interest in adventure and wife-hunting.

"Suppose," said Louhi thoughtfully, "suppose I could arrange for you to return home, what would you give me?"

"Oh, whatever you wish!" said Väinämöinen, suddenly cheerful. "A helmetful of gold, perhaps, or a hatful of silver?"

"Gold and silver are of little use to me," Louhi replied, "but there is something I'd like, very much. Life is hard here in the North Land, with all this ice and snow and darkness. If you could make me a . . . a Sampo, I'd gladly give you a horse and sledge for your journey home. And, what's more, I'd give you my daughter, for your wife, for I, old Louhi, am Mistress of the North, and the Maid of the North is my daughter!"

So, thought Väinämöinen, my journey has not been in vain, for here I am at the very house I thought I should never reach! But a Sampo! If I am to marry the Maid of the North, I must make her mother a Sampo!

"Dear Louhi," began Väinämöinen, wondering what to say, "I can't make a Sampo; but . . . but if you will get me home first, I'll send you somebody I know who can make one. His name is Ilmarinen. He's a smith. It was he who made the great dome of the sky, and there's not a single mark of his hammer upon it, so smoothly has he beaten it out. I'm sure he could make you a Sampo."

The old man is right, thought Louhi, there through the smoke-hole was the sky, with never a mark on it. This Ilmarinen must be the man for the job. "Very well, but remember," she said, helping Väinämöinen on with his coat, "I will only give my daughter to the man who makes me a Sampo."

She showed him out to the stable. "Here's a horse for you, and a sledge. Now, a word of warning," she went on, raising a crooked finger, "as you ride homewards, don't look about you until night has fallen—the horse knows the way. If you do look, you will suffer great woe!" And she drew the word out to make it sound as woeful as possible.

Off glided Väinämöinen in the sledge, speeding southward across the snow, his head bowed, thinking. Only the man who made the Sampo could marry the Maid of the North. Oh, he would get around that problem somehow; but let the Sampo be made first—he owed it to the old woman for the horse and sledge.

The Sampo. Life was hard, Louhi had said, but a Sampo would make all the difference. And what is a Sampo? The Tales tell us a great deal about the Sampo, that it was made by a smith and was therefore of metal, that it was gaily decorated with pictures, that it brought good fortune to its owner. They tell us that one of its uses was grinding corn to make flour, and that it had many other uses as well; but never, never do the Tales say exactly what the Sampo was, so we must be content with guessing.

What was that whirring, rattling noise? Väinämöinen recalled Louhi's warning but he could not resist looking about him to see where such a curious noise might be coming from. There was the snow, there were the forests, dim in the northern day, there was a lake; but he saw nothing that would ever make such a noise. It was like . . . it was like a shuttle going backward and forward across a loom as it wove cloth. Perhaps it was a bird, he thought. He looked above him—and could hardly believe his eyes.

There, in the sullen sky of the North Land, was a rainbow; but that was the least of wonders, for there, sitting on the rainbow if you please, was a girl—and the girl was weaving. There was her loom, and Väinämöinen could just see the shuttle flying to and fro, to and fro, as she passed it from one hand to the other.

Now, I need not tell you that it is not every girl who can sit on a rainbow, weaving. Väinämöinen realized that there was in fact only one girl who could do such a thing, and that was, yes, the Maid of the North, the beautiful, mysterious one whose name was never spoken.

"So that," he said under his breath, "is why Louhi told me not to look about me before nightfall. She doesn't want me to run off with her daughter before she has the Sampo!"

Does it seem strange that the girl who only a short

33

while ago was emptying a dustpan should now be sitting on a rainbow weaving? Even folk with such marvelous powers still have to do their housework.

"Maid of the North!" called Väinämöinen, checking his horse, "come down and sit beside me in my sledge."

"And why should the Maid of the North do such a thing?" she inquired loftily.

"To come home with me and be my wife," replied Väinämöinen, "and to share my house with me in fair Kalevala."

"A little bird told me," said the Maid of the North, "that to be a wife is to be a servant and wait upon an ungrateful husband. No, I'm quite happy as I am, thank you." And she went on with her weaving.

"The song of birds is so much idle chatter," answered the old man. "The unmarried girl is treated as a child by her parents, but a wife is regarded as a grown-up by all concerned. Come down into my sledge with me!"

"I will be your wife," said the Maid, "if you can split a horsehair with a blunt knife, and tie an egg in knots without the knots showing."

To anybody else this would be as good as saying no, but Väinämöinen climbed out of his sledge and plucked a hair out of the horse's tail. He got out the knife he always carried, and without sharpening it put the blade at one end of the hair. Steadily he ran it right down through the middle of the hair—and there were two hairs, so thin they could hardly be seen. Then he took an egg Louhi had given him for his lunch, and, without so much as a crack on its shell, it became the only egg that has ever been tied in knots.

"Now come down into my sledge!" he called, feeling delighted with himself.

"I will," said the Maid from her rainbow, "if you can peel this stone, and cut this block of ice without chipping it."

Väinämöinen took the stone and peeled it as if it had been a boiled turnip, then he cut the block of ice into pieces and there was not a chip or splinter to be seen.

"No sooner said than done," he declared, beaming. "Now come home with me."

"Gladly," said the Maid, "but first you must build a boat from the wood of my loom, and launch it on a lake without touching it."

"It so happens," said Väinämöinen with some pride, "that I am a master builder of boats. So if I may have your loom, please, I will get to work straight away."

The Maid of the North tossed her loom down to him and sat back on the rainbow to watch. Tying an egg in knots is one thing, but building a boat out of a small loom is quite another. She was looking forward to seeing the old fellow make a fool of himself.

Väinämöinen produced an enormous axe out of his sledge and started hacking at the loom with a will. Hour after hour he worked, chopping it into planks with which to build his boat. He might well have completed the task and swept the Maid of the North off her rainbow, but things turned out differently.

He was swinging his axe to make another plank when it slipped, struck the ground and bounced back, biting deep into his knee. He yelled as the blood gushed from the wound, and cursed the axe for not doing the job it was made for. Hopping about in agony he tried to think of a spell.

Suppose that you, like Väinämöinen, have cut your knee, and you want a spell for healing it. One thing is necessary; knowledge. What caused the damage? In this case, it was an axe. And what is an axe made of? Iron.

All you need to know is the Origin of iron, where it came from in the first place, and your troubles are over —or nearly so. Most people find that some ointment and a bandage come in useful as well; but it is the spell that counts really, for if you can tell the axe how it came to be an axe, it will be afraid you might send it back where it came from—and then there would be no axe. Imagine telling a troublesome stick that it was once part of a tree! The axe, or the stick, will be only too glad to undo what it has done, and your knee—plus some ointment and a bandage, mind—will soon be fit again.

Väinämöinen, then, tried to think of a spell as he nursed his knee. He sang all the songs of Origin he could think of, but the shame of it was he simply could not remember the Origin of iron. Perhaps he could not because of the pain, in any case, because he could not, the pain raged on.

As for the Maid of the North, nobody knows what happened to her. She offered no help to the injured old man, that much is certain. No doubt she floated away on her rainbow, sulking because she was no longer the center of attention, but we have not seen the last of her by any means.

Väinämöinen climbed painfully back into his sledge, shook the horse's reins, and glided off in search of somebody who might know the Origin of iron and dress his wound. He went one way and found a house, but nobody there could help him. He went another way and found another house, where an old woman lived; only three teeth she had in her ancient head, and the three teeth only lisped out the same answer.

Going a third way he was lucky. He found a cottage where an old man lived with his son. Looking at Väinämöinen's knee, the old man said wisely; "Greater floods than this have been stemmed. I'll see what I can do."

He helped Väinämöinen into his cottage and sat him down by the fire.

"An axe wound, you say?" asked the old man. "Mm . . . and a deep one too. Well, my friend, I can clean it out and put something on it, but first we must stop the bleeding—and I'm afraid I don't know the Origin of iron."

Then Väinämöinen remembered. At last he remembered the song of the Origin of iron. This is the curious story the song told.

Mother Nature had three sons; the eldest was called

Water, the middle one was called Fire and the youngest was called Iron. One day Iron went to visit his brother Fire. Now Fire was usually warm-natured, but at times he could get quite heated. On this particular day he was in a very bad mood, and as Iron approached he sprang at him and nearly ate him up. Poor Iron ran away and hid himself in the marshes and under the mountains, to keep out of Fire's way. But he soon grew bored with hiding in the dark; he wented to make himself useful. Hoping that his brother had cooled down a little since their last meeting, he decided to visit Fire again. Fire was living now with Ilmarinen, the smith.

When Ilmarinen saw Iron he said; "Come and meet your brother Fire"—and threw him into the flames.

"Help! Help!" screamed Iron. "Fire is eating me up. Save me!"

"But Iron," said Ilmarinen, "if I pull you out, you may be so hot and angry yourself that you will do some harm, or even kill your brother Fire."

"I promise," Iron gasped, "that if you pull me out I will do only useful things like cutting down trees and breaking rocks—but please hurry!"

Ilmarinen pulled Iron out of the flames and made him into axes, knives and other tools; but then he said to himself, "This Iron is too soft for really hard work. I will take him to his brother Water, who will make him tougher and stronger."

Ilmarinen took Iron along to Water; but Water was

also in a bad mood and refused to co-operate. At that moment a bee came buzzing around.

"O bee," called Ilmarinen politely, "go and bring me some honey, to sweeten this bitter Water."

Off flew the bee; but it was a wicked bee, and instead of bringing honey it brought poison from snakes and acid from red ants. Ilmarinen took what the bee had brought, poured it into the Water, stirred, and dipped the wretched Iron in the mixture.

"And that," said Väinämöinen, "is why Iron has bitten me today, because he was tempered in the poison of snakes and the acid of red ants."

"A bad temper indeed," said the old man, shaking his head. "O wretched Iron," he went on, turning to Väinä-möinen's wound, "misbehaving in this evil manner! For so long you were just poor little Iron, whom everyone felt sorry for. And what happens? No sooner have you found yourself a useful job of work and won our re-spect, than you grow too pleased with yourself and spoil it all, biting this good man who never did you any harm! I wonder what your family would say if they knew what you've done—eh? Now, stop hurting our friend here this minute, or I shall go straight and tell them— and you'll be in trouble! And as for you, O blood, you will be much happier flowing inside our friend's veins than running down his leg!"

When we say that something worked like a charm, we mean that it worked as this one did. The bleeding stopped, and Väinämöinen's knee left off hurting him. The old man sent his son out for some herbs, to make an ointment, while he filled a cauldron with water and hung it over the fire. The son came back with honey, oak twigs, green grass—all went into the cauldron, which boiled and bubbled busily.

After what seemed days the ointment was ready. All that remained was to test it, to make sure it was strong enough. The old man's son took some of it out across a field to where a slender aspen tree stood. He seized the tree and snapped it in half; then he smeared a little of the ointment on the broken trunk, and in the twinkling of an eye the tree was whole again and sturdier than before. On broken stones and cracked rocks too he tried it, and even they were healed. The young man returned to the cottage and told his father what the ointment had done. The old man dipped his finger in it and tasted it: yes, it was perfect.

Gently he rubbed the ointment into Väinämöinen's knee. Then he fetched some silken cloth, and cut it into strips with which he bound up the wound.

"I've learned my lesson," said Väinämöinen, gingerly bending his leg and standing up, "and that is, never to brag about my skill as a boat builder!"

And while the old man and his son were still wondering what he meant, Väinämöinen had thanked them both and continued on his way to the house of Ilmarinen, the maker of the Sampo.

THE SAMPO

here have you been all this time?" asked Ilmarinen, as his old friend appeared at the door of his smithy one evening. Ilmarinen—Sky-Maker—was a young and handsome craftsman. There was nobody in Kalevala, or in the North Land either, so clever as he with hammer and anvil. All around the walls of the smithy hung gleaming axes, knives and dozens of other tools he had made with the help of iron, fire and water—those three brothers of the song.

"I've been to the North Land," said Väinämöinen. "Ilmarinen, there's so much to tell you, I hardly know where to start. You've never been to the North Land, have you? You really ought to go, you know. It's a delightful place, and as for the Maid of the North—well, she's the most beautiful girl I've ever seen!"

Ilmarinen turned back to his work. Old Väinämöinen was always talking about beautiful girls! Ilmarinen was much more at home in his smithy, making tools by himself. He might get married one day, he thought, but he was quite happy on his own for the present.

"Yes," Väinämöinen went on eagerly. "Why don't you go to the North Land? There's an old woman there called Louhi—she's the Maid's mother and she says she'll only let her daughter marry the man who can make her a Sampo and . . ." He ran out of breath and stopped.

Ilmarinen stopped hammering and looked up. "But I'm the only man who can make a Sampo."

Väinämöinen nodded, hoping that Ilmarinen would see what he had in mind.

"Knowing you, old friend," said Ilmarinen with a smile, "I expect you've already told this Louhi that I will make her a Sampo."

Väinämöinen shifted from one foot to the other, uncertain what to say.

"Mm, I thought so," said Ilmarinen without waiting for a reply. "And I dare say too that I'm as good as married to this wonderful daughter of hers."

Väinämöinen said nothing, but turned a deep red under his white beard—not so much because Ilmarinen had guessed the right answer, but because he wanted to marry the Maid of the North himself. One thing was for sure, though, Louhi would not let her out of her sight until she had the Sampo well and truly under lock and key.

"No!" said Ilmarinen, so loudly that Väinämöinen jumped. "No, I won't go to the North Land, not even to please you! And do you know why? I've heard," he said darkly, "that the people of the North Land go around eating each other—and that's no place for me!"

It was obvious that Ilmarinen simply did not want to go. Väinämöinen stroked his beard and pondered a moment.

"Ilmarinen," he said suddenly.

But Ilmarinen had gone back to his anvil and was banging away with his hammer again.

"ILMARINEN!" shouted Väinämöinen above the din. Ilmarinen put his hammer down with a crash.

"What is it now?" he asked impatiently.

"Ilmarinen, have you ever seen a tree with the moon and the stars sitting in its branches like birds?"

"No," he growled, "and nor have you."

"Oh, but I have," Väinämöinen insisted, "and what's more, in this very land of ours—and not far from here, either."

"I don't believe you," said Ilmarinen, less impatient and rather curious in spite of himself.

"Just you come with me, then," said Väinämöinen gleefully, "and I'll show you."

What is the old rascal up to now? Ilmarinen wondered, wiping the soot off his hands and putting on his coat. So far so good! thought Väinämöinen, rubbing his hands together as he led Ilmarinen out into the clear night. Along a narrow path they went, Väinämöinen first with Ilmarinen close behind. The little procession picked its way through the darkness and came to a halt at the edge of a cornfield where a tall, solitary pine tree stood. Without a word Väinämöinen pointed upward.

Great craftsman though he was, Ilmarinen was quite simple minded in many ways. There, just as his friend had said, was the moon—and there were the stars too—

sitting in the branches of the tree like so many birds. He looked around at Väinämöinen, and blinked at him.

"Go on, then," said Väinämöinen, keeping as straight a face as he could, "climb up and bring them down!"

Quite bewildered, Ilmarinen swung himself up into the pine tree and began climbing to where he had seen the moon and the stars. And Väinämöinen began singing . . .

All of a sudden a wind sprang up, a wild, howling wind that shook the pine tree to its very roots; and to the wind Väinämöinen sang:

> *"Take him up, wind, in your vessel*
> *bear him in your boat, O weather*
> *gustily aboard convey him*
> *to the grim and gloomy North Land!"*

The wind grew still wilder, and howling it swept poor Ilmarinen out of the tree away into the sky. Over the snowclad forests he flew, gasping for breath, across the icy lakes, and he landed with a thump right outside Louhi's gate.

"Oh, and which way did you come?" asked old Louhi in amazement. "I didn't hear the watchdogs bark."

"The way I came," replied Ilmarinen, quickly recovering himself, "your watchdogs wouldn't have heard me. That's why you didn't hear him."

Louhi was puzzled. "Well, anyway," she said, "how-

44

ever you came, did you by chance hear or see anything of Ilmarinen, the great smith and cunning craftsman? We've been expecting him for some time. You see," she explained, "he's supposed to be coming to forge a Sampo for us."

"Why, yes," said Ilmarinen, "now that you mention it, I have heard the name. In fact, I met him on my way here. I"—he paused for effect—"am Ilmarinen, the great smith and cunning craftsman you speak of."

Hardly staying to welcome her visitor, old Louhi scuttled off indoors. Trailing behind her, Ilmarinen heard her talking excitedly to somebody, but did not catch what she was saying.

"Come along, daughter," she was saying, "get yourself up in your best clothes. Best dress, best necklace, earrings—and put on some make-up. Ilmarinen's here— you know, Ilmarinen—the one who's going to make our Sampo . . . Ah, there you are," she said as Ilmarinen caught up with her, "dinner's waiting. This way, please. Nothing but the best for Ilmarinen!" And she sat him down before a gigantic meal.

Some time later Ilmarinen leaned back from the table and loosened his belt. He could not recall having eaten and drunk quite so much before. This North Land was not so bad after all.

"Ilmarinen," began Louhi when she saw that he was well at ease in his new surroundings, "you are, we know, a great smith and a cunning craftsman. Now, how

45

would you like the most beautiful girl in all the world as your wife? She is yours, if you will make us a Sampo. I've all the ingredients you'll need—the wing tips of white swans, the milk of a cow that has no calf, a grain of barley, a few shreds of wool."

"Then I will," said Ilmarinen. "I will make your Sampo. It was I, you know, who made the vault of the sky, so a Sampo is no problem at all."

Next day he set to work looking for a suitable place to build a forge—a hole in which to make a fire, and a large boulder to use as an anvil on which to beat out the softened iron. After much searching he found a patch of rocky ground, and with the help of some men Louhi had sent out with him he lit a huge fire and prepared some bellows.

For three days and three nights the men piled up fuel on the fire and worked the bellows. The special ingredients were thrown in, and Ilmarinen looked down into the flames to see what was taking shape.

Rising out of the glowing depths of the fire was a bright crossbow, tipped with silver and with a shaft of copper. But Ilmarinen knew it to be an evil crossbow, which would thirst for human blood, so he broke it in pieces and threw the pieces back in the fire.

"Work the bellows harder!" he called to the men. The fire roared, and Ilmarinen looked down into it again.

Coming up out of the flames was a boat, a magnificent

red boat with copper trimmings. But Ilmarinen knew it to be an evil boat, which would go to war, so he smashed it in splinters and threw the splinters back.

"Harder, harder work the bellows!" he called to the men. The fire roared louder; Ilmarinen had another look, and saw a cow, a marvelous cow with golden horns. But Ilmarinen knew it to be a lazy cow, which would sleep all day and lose its milk, so he cut it in fragments and cast the fragments back in the flames.

"Work the bellows harder still!" he called to the men. The fire roared louder still, and Ilmarinen looked once more. This time there was a plough of copper with a ploughshare of gold, a frame of copper and handles tipped with silver. But Ilmarinen knew it to be an evil plough, which would plough up ripe cornfields and green meadows, so he broke it in pieces and hurled the pieces back. Then he lifted his head and addressed the sky.

"O winds," he called, "work these bellows as they've never been worked before!"

The four winds rose and screamed with all their force. Never was there seen such a fire. The flames scorched upward, the smoke billowed into the sky. Ilmarinen looked down through the terrifying heat, and there— there at the bottom of the furnace he saw the Sampo slowly forming.

When it was soft enough he drew it out, and hammered it and beat it with all his strength and skill till it

47

was finished, complete with fantastic decorations all over it. One side of it was a corn mill, another was a salt mill, and a third was a mill for coining money; but what it was altogether nobody knows any more.

Ilmarinen took it back to Louhi, who immediately set it to work. She laughed with delight as it churned and turned and twisted; but she could see that many people would be only too eager to make off with it. She had it carried to her storehouse in the Copper Mountain among the hills of the North Land, where she had it locked behind nine great locks and rooted down with three mighty roots.

Ilmarinen had been thinking about the Maid of the North. True, he was not so much in need of a wife as his friend Väinämöinen seemed to be, but, as he had told him, he intended to get married one fine day. Now, he thought, this was as fine a day as had ever come up behind the trees. Here was the most beautiful girl in the world, and she was his for the asking! Yes, he decided, it was time he had a wife after all. But he was in for a disappointment.

"Mistress Louhi," he said, "now that I've made the Sampo, may I take your daughter as my wife?"

Before Louhi had a chance to say anything, the Maid of the North, who had been keeping herself very much to herself till now, said: "And leave all my berries un-plucked on the hills, leave my meadows and forests un-visited? Oh no. I'm far from ready yet to leave my home for a foreign country."

A big, black cloud seemed to descend over Ilmarinen's face. Louhi was quite at a loss for a moment.

"Er . . . Ilmarinen," she said, "you're looking very downcast. Are . . . are you homesick, perhaps?"

"Yes, homesick . . . that's what I am," Ilmarinen replied.

"I shall have something to say to you, my girl, when the young man's gone," said Louhi, glaring at her daughter.

And that was all. Louhi gave Ilmarinen a good meal, and put him in a boat, and wished him a safe journey home.

"Welcome home," said Väinämöinen when he was back in Kalevala. "And did you make the Sampo?"

"Yes," sighed Ilmarinen, "I made the Sampo."

THE DEVIL'S HORSE

 magine a tall young man with hair as yellow as a barley field at harvest time and eyes as blue and as deep as a lake which reflects the sky, a skilled hunter and fisherman, a restless maker of mischief and a great chaser of pretty girls— and you are thinking of Lemminkäinen. Lemminkäinen—Lover-Man—lived with his mother, a wise old woman who thought the world of him, on one of those thousands of forest-covered islands which are dotted about the long lakes of Kalevala.

"Mother," he said one day, "I've a mind to go northward. I'll go and fight the men of the North Land and —who knows?—if one of their women should take my fancy, I'll carry her off and make her my wife."

"Silly boy!" his mother warned him. "The men of the North Land are wiser and stronger than you. They'll sing their songs at you and you'll find yourself roasting over a fire!"

"Ha! And do you think I'm afraid of their songs?" he laughed. "Do you know, Mother, three of those fine Northmen tried their songs out on me once. There they stood, all through one summer night, perched on a rock singing. I think they were trying to sink me in a bog or something. They certainly got what was coming to them. I hope they're comfortable now, lying under the waterfall of the Black River!"

"It'll be the death of you, my lad, if you go," said his

mother, taking no notice of his stories—she knew him of old. But Lemminkäinen was already brushing his hair.

"Look, Mother," he said, throwing the hairbrush down, "if anything happens to me, that brush will start bleeding—so there!"

And he put on his coat of mail, took his sword, and was off on his sledge before the old woman could say another word.

After a long, cold ride he reached the North Land and drew to a halt at Louhi's gate. He climbed out of his sledge and stood in the snow, listening; had anybody seen him or heard him come? No, all was quiet except for a hubbub of chatter and singing from inside the house.

He crept up to a window and peered in. Oh! There were more people than he had expected—and they were nearly all singers! Lemminkäinen knew he could deal with any number of warlike young men, however strong they might be. It was a simple matter of wielding his sword; but singers—and so many of them! He knew a few songs himself, but they would hardly stand up to the powerful wisdom of these older men.

He stood outside the window, wondering what to do. Yes, he decided, the best thing was first to change his shape into something so small that he could get in unnoticed; then to change back into himself and see what happened. After all, he had not come this far for nothing.

"All this noise!" he shouted when he was inside the

house. "The best part of any song is the end of it! Better still is not to sing at all!"

The singers stopped. Who was this rude young man, and how had he got in? Old Louhi stalked up to him in a rage.

"What have you done with the watchdogs, for them not to hear you and warn us?" she stormed.

"I'm not so stupid as to come charging in here and get bitten by your dogs," said Lemminkäinen, looking around at everybody. I can manage this crowd, he thought, and he went on; "When I was a small boy my mother taught me some of her songs. Listen—and watch!"

He started to sing, and before his song was over there was not a man left in the place. Far away, here in a lake, there on a treeless plain in the far north, singers who a moment ago were sitting in the warmth of Louhi's hearth were rubbing their eyes and scratching their heads, wondering what had happened to them.

Not a man left? There was, in fact, one man left in Louhi's house that day. He was a very old man, a cowherd, and quite blind. His name was Märkähattu—Dripcap. A strange name? Not so, as we shall see.

"How is it, my fine young fellow," he squeaked, "that you have not sent me away, along with all the other men?"

"You?" Lemminkäinen sneered. "And why should I send you away? What have I to fear from a blind old fool who can't even see the cattle he's supposed to look after?" And he gave the old fellow a great slap on the back that sent him sprawling.

Märkähattu picked himself up, grinding his teeth in fury. He would show this young scoundrel just what he had to fear from him. He stumbled off, feeling his way, to a river he knew—the Black River of Tuonela, the kingdom of death. Lemminkäinen would be passing there on his way home; he would have his revenge of him then.

"Mistress Louhi," said Lemminkäinen meanwhile, "give me your daughter, the Maid of the North, to be my wife."

"To a conceited puppy like you?" said Louhi, in an even greater rage. "Not unless you can catch me the Elk of Hiisi—the Devil's Elk; and you must hunt it on foot, with only skis to help you along."

To anybody else this was as good as saying no, you can't marry my daughter, but Lemminkäinen sharpened his spear, made himself a strong new crossbow and tipped his arrows with sharp pieces of bone. All he needed now was a pair of skis. Without skis he could only plod about, knee deep in snow at the best of times; while at the forest he might fall into a crevasse between rocks, which the snow had covered over. So he went to a ski maker and told him of his purpose.

"Hunting the Elk of Hiisi?" laughed the ski maker. "You must be mad, my friend. All you'll get for your pains is a lump of rotten timber."

Nevertheless he made the skis for Lemminkäinen,

planing the wood till it was smooth, fixing on tough leather straps and rubbing in reindeer fat to make the skis swift and supple. Lemminkäinen stepped into them, slung spear, crossbow and quiver on his back, and thrust himself forward with his pole.

"No living creature," he called to the frozen landscape as he dashed along, "is safe from me!"

Somewhere, in dreadful haunts where no man has ever ventured, Hiisi himself heard the young man's boasting, and with all his wicked skill formed an elk for his hunting. The elk is a cousin to the reindeer, but it is larger and roams wild in the wastes of the north; but this was the Devil's Elk, more terrifying than any other beast on earth. Its head was of rotten timber, with spreading antlers of willow branches. Its feet were made of the tough reeds which men plait into ropes, and its legs were sticks pulled out of marshes. Its back was sturdily built of poles with which men make fences, and its sinews were of tough, dry grass. Its staring eyes were the huge flowers of the water lily, whose broad leaves formed its ears. Its hide was of the bark of the pine tree, and its flesh, like its head, was of rotten timber. This was the vile creature which Hiisi fashioned for Lemminkä- inen to hunt, not living but fleeter of foot than anything of flesh and blood.

When Hiisi had let it loose the Elk sped away toward the North Land, running like clockwork across the snow-covered plains, tearing through people's farms and backyards, kicking over tubs and cooking-pots and everything that lay in its path. Men shouted and dogs barked; there had never been such a commotion in that silent, gloomy land.

Lemminkäinen was dashing along over hills and marshes looking for the Elk. No sign of it yet; he drove his ski pole into the snow and hurried on.

What was the noise? In the distance he saw a farm, men and dogs were running about, shouting and barking. He went closer and asked what the trouble was.

"Trouble enough," said the people at the farm. "The Elk of Hiisi has passed this way. Look, it has spilled all our water and knocked our dinner into the fire."

So he was heading in the right direction! On he went, pushing on his pole, gliding over the white ground, and before long he caught up with the beast. Working quickly and quietly he made a collar of birch wood, which he fastened on the end of a long stick. Then he came alongside of the Elk, and with a leap flung the collar around its neck.

"Got you!" he panted, dragging it to a halt. He drove the stick into the ground and pulled some fallen boughs of an oak tree into a circle around it.

"You just stay here for a while, my beauty," he said to it, patting its wooden back, "and don't be in such a hurry!"

Now, how was he going to get this creature back to Louhi and claim his prize? The Elk saw that Lemminkäinen was distracted for a moment and took its chance. Suddenly it wrenched its neck free of the collar, charged through its pen of oak boughs, and before Lemminkäinen had realized what had happened it was whirring and clanking on its way once more.

Wearily Lemminkäinen took up the chase again, but he had not gone far when his left ski caught in a hole and snapped in half, and as he tried to recover his balance he tripped over his right ski and broke that too. Then, and worst of all, he fell against his spear and snapped it.

Without skis, without spear, what was he to do? He could not bear the thought of returning to Louhi without the Elk, but how could he catch it now? He limped sadly across the snow and wandered into a forest.

"Ukko," he called to the Lord of the Weather and the Chief of Spirits, "may it please you to make me a new pair of skis and a new spear, so that I can continue my hunt for the Devil's Elk! Tapio, Lord of the Forests, I call to you; guide me to my quarry!"

Half shouting, half singing, he called to all the kindly forest spirits as he walked beneath the tall, still trees, but there was not a single answer to his cries. After wandering many miles he stumbled up a hill in the middle of the forest. From its summit he saw, away to the northwest, the group of huts which he knew to be Tapiola, the dwelling-place of Tapio. He broke into a run and hastened down the other side of the wooded hill towards the huts.

"Good Tapio, and you, gracious Mistress of the Forests," he called when he reached them, "with your power guide the Elk of Hiisi into this great forest and help me to catch it! I have broken my skis and my spear, and I have wandered footsore for many miles." And remembering he had some money in his purse, he went on:

> ". . . *Master of the house of Tapio*
> *Mistress of the house of Tapio*
> *aged greybeard of the forest*
> *golden king of all the forest!*
> *Mimerkki, the forest's mistress*
> *bounteous and beloved old woman*
> *blue robed lady of the thickets*
> *red socked mistress of the marshes!*
> *Come, with me your gold to barter*
> *and with me to change your silver.*
> *I have gold as old as moonlight*
> *silver ancient as the sunlight . . .*"

The Master and Mistress of Tapiola were charmed with this respectful young man. They gave him a new pair of skis and a new spear, and sent him singing through the forest in search of the Elk once more. Of course, with their mysterious help he soon found it, and this time he lassoed it with a good strong rope. He shouted his thanks through the echoing woodland and started off for Louhi's farm, dragging the Elk behind him.

"Mistress, I've caught the Devil's Elk for you," Lemminkäinen announced. "Now give me your daughter."

"I will only give you my daughter," said Louhi, scheming as ever, "if you can bridle the Devil's Horse for me."

Without another word Lemminkäinen seized a bridle finely decorated with gold and silver, and went off in search of the Horse of Hiisi. For two days he traveled and found nothing; then on the morning of the third day he climbed a hill to have a look around. There in the east, where the sun was rising, he saw a proud horse kicking and stamping among the trees. It was the Devil's Horse, he could see, for it was breathing smoke and its mane was a mass of yellow fire.

That was the problem indeed; how to get near enough to bridle it, without being burned to cinders?

Easy, thought Lemminkäinen with a grin; and he began singing:

> *"Ukko, you of gods the highest*
> *Ukko, you of clouds the keeper*
> *of the scattered clouds director!*
> *Throw your sky-blue portals open*
> *all the windows of the weather*
> *hurl down hailstones all of iron*
> *and release an icy deluge*
> *on the mane of that good stallion*
> *on the rump of Hiisi's courser!"*

The sky grew overcast. First a few drops came, then a few more. Heavier and heavier they fell, larger and larger, until huge lumps of hail came hurtling down, a flood of frozen rain. And right in the middle of the storm stood the Devil's Horse, giving off clouds of steam.

Now, the Devil's Horse is a terrible beast, with its mane of fire; but when the fire is put out, it is as mild as any horse that draws a sledge. Lemminkäinen ran whooping down the hillside over to the trees where it was standing, and calmly as you like he fixed the bridle on its head. The horse, still steaming and quite bewildered, let itself be mounted and ridden back to Louhi with no trouble at all.

"Here is your Devil's Horse, Mistress," said Lemminkäinen triumphantly. "I hope it will be company for the Devil's Elk. May I have your daughter now?"

"Not so fast, young man," said Louhi. "One more job you must do for me before I give you my daughter. On the River of Tuonela lives a great white swan, with a single arrow you must shoot the Swan of Tuonela."

Lemminkäinen took up his crossbow and his quiver, and set out for the kingdom of Tuoni, the Lord of Death. The land grew darker as he journeyed, until he reached the caverns of Tuonela where the river ran black and deep under a waterfall.

Lemminkäinen peered about him in the frightening gloom, a white swan should not be difficult to find, he thought. The loneliest place in the world, perhaps—if it is really in the world. Lemminkäinen shuddered. He had never felt so lonely before.

Lonely, but not alone. Under the waterfall somebody was waiting for him. Märkähattu—Dripcap, the old, blind cowherd, had been waiting a long time for his young enemy, and now he heard him from where he was hiding. With all the secret power his old age gave him he sent a snake up out of the swirling river towards the unsuspecting Lemminkäinen. The snake lashed viciously at the young man's flesh, and plunged its fangs deep into his heart.

He staggered and slumped to the ground. Inches away the dreadful river rippled and chuckled. Lemminkäinen knew no words to soothe the bite of water snakes; how he wished that he had taken his mother's advice and not gone on this ridiculous expedition, or that he had at least gained a little more wisdom before he had left!

Märkähattu stumbled out from under the waterfall and groped his way to where Lemminkäinen was lying. With a mighty effort he picked the young man up in his arms, stood a moment swaying in the darkness with him, and flung him into the river. Lemminkäinen was too weak to struggle as the eddying waters tossed him about and spun him around, as though they were uncertain what to do with him. Märkähattu drew his sword, leaned out over the river, and hacked blindly at the water where he guessed Lemminkäinen would be.

He guessed rightly. The pieces of Lemminkäinen's

body swirled around once more before being sucked down into the black river's depth.

"Shoot as many swans as you like now, young fellow!" Märkähattu cackled, shambling off into the darkness.

"I wonder what's become of that son of mine?" said Lemminkäinen's mother to herself as she went about her housework. "Weeks have gone by and still there's no sign of him."

She stood her broom in a corner and took a duster into his room. She was dusting the table by his bed, when his hairbrush caught her gaze. There was something different about it; but what could it be? She picked it up to have a closer look.

It . . . it was bleeding! The hairbrush was bleeding! She suddenly recalled what Lemminkäinen had said: that if anything happened to him . . .

"He's in trouble!" she cried, dropping hairbrush and duster; and lifting up her long skirts she ran down to the lakeside, rowed over to the mainland and ran on— through the forests, over the mountains, across the valleys, her aged feet pounding away—until at length this remarkable old woman reached the North Land and was hammering on Louhi's gate.

"Mistress of the North," she panted, "where is my son, where have you sent him?"

"I haven't the faintest idea where your son is," replied Louhi. "I gave him a horse and a sledge, and he left here not long ago, but where he's gone I can't say. If you haven't seen him," she added wickedly, "perhaps he has been devoured by wolves in the forests."

"That's a shameless lie!" screamed Lemminkäinen's mother. "No wolf could touch my boy, he'd kill it with his bare hands. Now, tell me what has happened to him, or I will smash your precious Sampo."

"I gave him a good meal, and he went off in a boat; but what has become of him I can't guess—unless he has been drowned."

"That's a lie too!" said Lemminkäinen's mother. She knew that her son was too clever a sailor to drown. "Now, tell me where you've sent him, or it'll be the worse for you."

"Very well," said Louhi. "First I sent him elk hunting, then I sent him to bridle a horse, and now he's shooting swans somewhere. I really don't know if anything has happened to him, but he hasn't come back yet to claim my daughter as his wife."

High and low, in marshes, on plains, around jutting headlands, along lakeshores Lemminkäinen's mother searched for her son, in vain. She asked a pine tree whether he had passed by; but the pine was too upset with the thought of being chopped down one day to bother with anything else. She asked the path she was walking on; but the path was too troubled with the thought of being forever trampled down by man and beast to worry about other matters. She asked the moon in the evening; but the moon was so sorry for itself, wandering in the lonely sky, that it did not notice anything that went on below. In the morning she asked the sun; and the sun, which sees all things, told her how her son was lost in the black river of Tuonela. She lifted up her skirts again and pounded off southward to the forge of Ilmarinen.

"Ilmarinen, great smith," she cried, "make me a long, wide rake with a copper handle and teeth of steel!"

Ilmarinen did not ask any questions, though he must have wondered what an old woman would want with such an enormous rake—some say its teeth were over six hundred feet long and its handle thirty feet long. When the rake was finished Lemminkäinen's mother ran back with it toward Tuonela.

"O brilliant sun!" she called as she ran, "shine out upon the darkness of Tuoni's kingdom, and lull the evil ones to sleep for a while!"

The sun stepped down out of the sky, leveled its beams through the dark caverns for a moment, then climbed back into its lofty place; and while the whole of death's kingdom dozed in its first and last noonday Lemminkäinen's mother ran down to the murky river.

Toward her and away, toward her and away went the rake through the waters near the bank; and found nothing. The old woman leaped into the river up to her waist, and drew the rake through the deeper water

63

farther out. Toward her and away she combed once more, under the cataract and out into the rushing gloom.

All of a sudden the rake caught on something. She tugged and heaved, her heart beating fast. Here was a shirt . . . her son's shirt! She pulled it off the prongs and threw it behind her on to the bank. Toward her and away went the rake. Here was his hat . . . and his stockings!

She waded still farther from the bank, quite unaware of the awful danger, and struck out afresh. Ah, here was something heavier. She dragged at the rake with all her might, and slowly, painfully out of the depths rose Lemminkäinen's body, limp and unmoving on the long teeth of the rake.

She carried him lovingly in her arms to the bank, where she had put his clothes. Struggling out of the water herself she looked at her son, and saw with bitter sorrow the work of Märkähattu's sword.

"How, oh, how can this lifeless wreck become a man again?" she cried through her tears.

"Ha ha! Ha ha! It cannot! It cannot!" croaked a raven overhead. "Look where the sword has cut bits of him away! If I were wise enough to put life back into this carcass, I might make it into a fish, perhaps . . . but not a man!"

And still croaking to itself the raven swung off into the gloom.

The old woman did not lose heart. She took her rake and dragged the river once more. It is strange how the most frightful tasks lose much of their horror when they are done in love. It was with positive joy that she dredged up part of Lemminkäinen's head that was missing, one of his hands and pieces of his backbone and ribs.

With rare skill she put the fragments in place and drew the flesh together over them, singing all the while a powerful song:

> *"Gracious lady of the veinlets*
> *Suonetar, O gracious lady*
> *lovely weaver of the veinlets*
> *with your gracious wooden flax-rod*
> *with your distaff made of copper*
> *with your spinning-wheel of iron!*
> *Hither come when you are needed*
> *hither hasten at my calling*
> *in your lap a mesh of veinlets*
> *in your arms a sheaf of membranes*
> *for the binding of the veinlets*
> *for the tying of the vein ends*
> *where the wounds are cracked and open*
> *where the gashes still are gaping! ..."*

Lemminkäinen's mother sang on, calling to all the good spirits for help; to row a tiny boat up and down the bloodstream, through the shattered joints and the broken bones; to sew the veins together with silken thread; to drive a tiny sledge over the torn flesh, checking the flow of blood, setting the bones, knitting the skin together.

Gradually the limp form on the river bank came to look like Lemminkäinen once more, but still he lay motionless and without speech. The old woman looked up from her work, wondering what to do next, and she saw a bee hovering nearby.

"O bee, honey maker," she said, "fly to Tapiola, the forest kingdom, and bring me honey from the flowers in its glades, to make an ointment for my son's body!"

The bee flew off, and soon returned with honey freshly drawn from six bright flowers and a hundred sweet grasses. The old woman took it and rubbed it hopefully on her son's cold body; but he made no movement, nor did he utter a single word.

"O hard-working bee," the mother begged, "fly over nine lakes to a beautiful island where you will find flowers in plenty, and bring me their honey for my son!"

Off went the bee again, to the island where they gather honey into earthenware pots no bigger than your thumb. It was a long journey for such a small creature, but it did not stop even to rest its wings. Back it came to Tuonela, carrying seven tiny pots brimming with honey. The old woman took them and emptied them on her son's body; but it was still quite cold.

"O high-flying bee," she implored, "fly up now into the sky, and bring me honey from the calm fields of heaven. Surely an ointment from Ukko himself will work wonders on my son!"

The bee hesitated a moment, then gathering up its

minute strength it buzzed away, out of the caverns of death's kingdom, up, up into the places of light far above the earth. Following the old woman's directions it soared past the Hunter, beyond the Great Bear and the Seven Stars, to fetch the sweetest honey of all.

In a remarkably short time it was back from its dizzy voyage and offering its priceless cargo to Lemminkäinen's mother.

"Mm . . . this is it," said the old woman joyfully. "This is the ointment I need—the honey of heaven, which heals all suffering, even the suffering of death." And the bee was gone before she had time to thank it.

Tenderly, with strong, smooth hands she rubbed the salve on her son's body. All over she rubbed him, warming the chill flesh, quickening the still blood, and saying: "Rise, my son, from your sleep; wake up out of your dark dreams!"

Lemminkäinen's eyelids twisted and flickered; then he opened his eyes and yawned.

"O-oh, Mother," he yawned, "that was a long and troublesome sleep. Where am I?"

"If it hadn't been for me, my lad," said his mother, helping him to his feet, "you'd have slept even longer. Where are you? You're in Tuonela. Now, you tell me how you came to be in the river, I've been worried nearly out of my mind!"

"It was Märkähattu—old Dripcap the cowherd," Lemminkäinen explained. "He sent a water snake against me and I don't know any songs to protect me from water creatures."

"Brave, foolish boy!" laughed the old woman, hugging him. "Setting out to conquer the North Land, and not knowing the Origin of water snakes; Now, before we go, is there anything you want?"

"Yes, Mother, as a matter of fact there is," replied Lemminkäinen, quite himself again. "A girl from the North Land—that's what I want! But that nasty old woman won't give me her daughter till I shoot the Swan of Tuonela."

"Leave the poor bird alone!" said his mother, taking his arm, "and come along home with me. You don't know what a narrow escape you've had."

And home they went arm in arm together.

VÄINÄMÖINEN

T hings had not turned out so badly after all, thought Väinämöinen, stroking his beard. Ilmarinen had forged the Sampo, but the Maid of the North had refused to marry him—for the time being, anyway. Väinämöinen had expected the Maid to fall in love with his handsome young friend immediately, which would have meant a quick journey to the North Land for the old man and a few last-minute spells if nothing else worked; but there was no need for all that now. While the Maid was making up her mind whether or not to marry after all, and then perhaps deciding on a husband, he had time to think of a really good plan and carry it out properly.

Well, he had thought of a plan—a really good one too. He would build a magnificent boat, sail to the North Land, show off his wisdom and skill to the Maid, marry her and bring her home while Ilmarinen was still waiting for her to change her mind!

Now if he was to impress the Maid, it must be a boat such as had never been seen before. First, it must be of the strongest oak, to withstand the most violent storms. Who would know where to find the strongest oak? Why, of course—that tiny, copper-clad man who had felled the great oak for him long ago, the oak which had been shutting off the sun from the earth at the beginning of time.

Sampsa Pellervoinen was his name, for he watched over *pellot*—the fields; and at Väinämöinen's bidding he set off, axe on shoulder, to find the strongest oak. On the way he passed an aspen tree, and wondered whether that would do instead.

"I'm no good for boat building," sighed the slender aspen, its branches trembling in the breeze. "I'm full of insects, which have gnawed me hollow."

Sampsa Pellervoinen went a little further and saw a pine tree. Perhaps the pine tree would do.

"Oh no, not I," said the pine sadly. "A raven has croaked in my branches, and I should bring misfortune."

At length Sampsa Pellervoinen came upon an oak tree.

"I'm delighted to help," said the oak grandly. "The sun has shone through me by day, and by night the moon has smiled on my leaves. What's more, the cuckoo itself has paid me a visit."

Sampsa Pellervoinen felled the oak, chopped it into planks and took the planks to Väinämöinen. The old man lavished all his care on the building of the boat, all his wisdom and skill. As wondrous songs poured from his lips, the planks rose, and bent themselves into the shape of a boat—keel, sides and rudder, gracefully curved, strong.

There, the boat was nearly finished. Väinämöinen paused and stepped back to look at his work. All it needed now was a few words to add the final touches.

He began singing once more, and suddenly stopped. How did it end, the song which was to complete the building of the boat? He sang the part he had just sung again, hoping that the song would carry itself over the part he had forgotten; but no, the song came to a dead stop at exactly the same place. Three words, three last words they were, to end the song and finish the boat, and they escaped him! What was he to do? He tried yet once more, going back to an earlier part of the song, trilling the well-known phrases for all he was worth—and stopped dead, precisely where he had stopped before.

Well, he must find the missing words, or his boat was useless and he would be without a wife. He went and sought them in all voices of nature; he asked the birds and the beasts of lake, field and forest, and though they chirped and bellowed at him not one of them told him the words he needed.

"I know where I'm certain to find them," said Väinä-möinen, "and it looks as though I shall have to go there after all." He meant Tuonela, the kingdom of death, which guards all the secrets of the living. He set out for Tuoni's dark dwelling, and in time he reached the bank of the river where Lemminkäinen had tried to shoot the swan.

"O daughter of Tuoni," he called into the darkness, "bring a boat and row me across into your kingdom!"

The hideous, stunted daughter of Tuoni heard him as she did her washing in the black water on the opposite bank. She stopped a moment and called back, "What brings you here, O man, if you are not dead? Only those who have departed from life are allowed into the kingdom of death."

"Tuoni himself has dragged me here," called Väinämöinen, trying to sound convincing.

"Liar! If Tuoni had brought you he would be with you, and I know he is not. Tell the truth now, what brings you here?"

"Iron it is, which has brought me here," called the old man. "I have been killed by the sword."

"Liar! If iron had brought you your clothes would be stained with blood, and I know they are not."

Väinämöinen tried again. "It was water," he called. "I have been drowned."

"Liar!" the voice insisted. "If water had brought you your clothes would be dripping wet, and I know they are not."

"It was fire, then. I have been burned to death."

"Liar! Liar! If fire had brought you your beard would be singed, and I know it is not. Now make an end to your stories and tell me truly why you have come."

"Very well," said Väinämöinen. "Yes, I have been misleading you. The fact is, I've been building a boat and I need a drill to mend a plank I've broken."

"Foolish man," cried the daughter of Tuoni, "coming to this kingdom while you are still living! Do not ask to come any further, for no man has returned from this side of the river alive!"

"Tell that to frightened old women," called Väinämöinen boldly, "but not to me! Now bring your boat
and row me across."

There was no reply, but soon he heard a creaking and
splashing in the darkness. It was a boat, rowed by the
ugliest young woman he had ever seen.

"Woe to you, Väinämöinen," she said as she helped
him aboard, "coming to Tuonela while the blood is still
warm in your veins!" And off they went across the
black water.

"Welcome, O Väinämöinen," said the aged Mistress
of Tuonela when he arrived. "Can I offer my guest a
drink to refresh him?" she smiled, handing him a tankard full of beer.

Väinämöinen took the tankard gratefully. He was
just about to lift it to his lips, when he saw that it was
thick with frog spawn and long, writhing worms.

"I have not come to death's kingdom to die of evil
beer," he declared scornfully, throwing the tankard on
the floor.

"Then why have you come, uncalled by Tuoni?" the
old woman asked.

"I was building a boat," replied Väinämöinen, "and
I found I needed three words—just three words—to
finish it. I sought them among the many voices of nature,
and because I didn't find them I came here."

"If we tell you the words you wish to know," said
the old woman, "you shall never return to the world
alive, for you will know the secrets of death."

73

Of what use are boats and wives to a dead man? Väinämöinen decided he must look elsewhere for his words, but he accepted the bed the old woman offered him, to rest before setting out on his homeward journey. But as he slept, the wicked son of Tuoni wove a net of iron which he let down into the river, to catch Väinämöinen when he tried to leave.

Väinämöinen did not sleep long that night, for this was a treacherous place in which to be off one's guard. He must be away before dawn. There was not much hope of his being ferried back across the river—in fact, it was unthinkable. So he changed himself into something long and thin, like a snake perhaps, and slithered through the night, through the dark waters, straight through the holes of the iron net without even noticing it . . . back into the land of the living, where he became an old man once more.

Early next morning the son of Tuoni went down to see what he had caught in his net; beautiful salmon there were, and smaller fish by the thousand, but not a single old man.

"So here I am, back where I started," said Väinämöinen to himself. "All that trouble for three words, and still I don't know them."

An aged shepherd overheard him. "I'm sure you will find them," he said, wagging a skinny finger, "and a good many more besides, in the mouth of the giant Antero Vipunen."

"And where," asked Väinämöinen, "shall I find the giant?"

"The road is difficult," said the shepherd, "but if you follow it you will arrive at him. The first part of the journey is over darning-needles, the second part is over sword blades, and the last part is over axes."

Väinämöinen thanked the shepherd for his guidance and pondered. This was a job for a smith, he thought, to make shoes that would walk over points and blades. He went to Ilmarinen, who made him a pair of tough iron shoes, and he was soon on his way, hopping over the darning-needles, skipping across the sword blades and jumping from one axe to another, till he arrived at Antero Vipunen—arrived at him, because the giant was huge enough to be a place.

Antero Vipunen was stretched out fast asleep. Now because a giant is so much bigger than a man, he needs that much more sleep. Antero Vipunen had been asleep for so long that a poplar tree was growing on his shoulders, a birch tree was standing on his forehead, an alder tree grew like a beard on his chin, and squirrels were scurrying about in his eyebrows.

Väinämöinen climbed up on to the giant. He felled the trees with his sword and drove the squirrels out of the giant's eyebrows. Then he thrust his sword into the giant's wide open, snoring mouth and waved it around inside, shouting, "Wake up, wake up, sleepyhead! I need your help."

Antero Vipunen opened one enormous, angry eye to see who was disturbing him. Väinämöinen was standing like a fly on his nose.

Either the giant sneezed, or Väinämöinen lost his footing, or something, for the next minute Väinämöinen was tumbling beard over iron shoes into Antero Vipunen's mouth. The giant gave a great gulp, and Väinämöinen was gone.

"Ho ho!" boomed Antero Vipunen. "I've eaten many dainty things in my time—sheep and goats, cows and pigs—but never have I tasted such a morsel as this!"

What was Väinämöinen to do? Standing inside the giant he stroked his beard and pondered once again. His knife! Of course, it was too small to be of any use as a cutting tool, but it had a wooden handle. With his skill as a boat builder Väinämöinen sang the knife's handle into a small boat complete with a pair of oars, which he rowed vigorously through the tracts and channels of the giant's belly.

Antero Vipunen did not even notice, or, if he did feel some movement, he probably thought it was a touch of indigestion after swallowing the old man whole. Väinämöinen abandoned the boat and stroked his beard again. Then he pulled off his shirt and trousers, and tied knots in them.

If anybody else had been inside the giant at the time, they would have wondered—quite understandably—what he was up to. A spark appeared from nowhere.

Väinämöinen fanned it with his shirt and trousers until it had grown into a flame; then he began hammering, using his elbow as a hammer and his knee as an anvil.

It is not a pleasant feeling to have a smith inside you, even if you are a giant. Antero Vipunen squirmed uncomfortably, and the smoke and fumes from the fire made him hiccough and swallow.

"What kind of man is this, to cause me such pain?" he grumbled; and he called down to Väinämöinen: "Come out of me, man! Leave me in peace!"

"Oh, but I rather like it here," came the reply, with more smoke and a few flames. "It's very warm—and well stocked with food, I see; whenever I'm hungry I can simply carve off a slice of giant."

Antero Vipunen groaned.

"Let me make a bargain with you," Väinämöinen went on. "I will stop hammering, if you will sing me all your wisdom. Then, perhaps, you will let me go, and I shall never disturb you again."

That sounds reasonable, thought the giant, and started singing. Day and night, day and night Antero Vipunen sang his songs of Origin, songs of air, water and earth, songs of the moon, the sun, the sky, the stars. The songs streamed from his mouth like so many horses at full gallop, their manes and tails flowing free. And barely noticeable amid the spate of four-footed spells came the three words Väinämöinen was listening for.

"And now," said Väinämöinen when the giant had

finished, "perhaps you will let me go, for I must be on my way."

"Gladly I will," said Antero Vipunen. "Many indeed are the dainties I've sampled, but none was quite like Väinämöinen. I was happy when you came, but, believe me, I shall be even happier when you've gone."

So saying Antero Vipunen opened his mouth wide, and Väinämöinen, clambering back into his shirt and trousers, hurried up from the giant's belly and out through his mouth homeward.

And in as little time as it takes to sing three words the boat was ready.

"I wonder what that is?" said a girl as she looked up from her washing at a lakeside. "That speck on the water—is it a bird, or a fish, or even a rock?"

But it was not a bird, nor was it a fish, nor even was it a rock. It was a boat—and what a superb boat it was too.

"Hei, Väinämöinen!" she called. "Where are you going this fine morning?"

Väinämöinen looked to see who was calling. Oh dear, it was Annikki, the sister of Ilmarinen. He had hoped he would pass by without being seen.

"I," he called back, "am going salmon fishing in the river of Tuonela."

"This isn't the season for salmon and well you know it, old man," said Annikki. "Now, tell me where you're going."

"I," came the answer, "am going to catch geese on the western lakes."

"Then where's your crossbow? And where's the dog to bring you the geese once you've shot them down?"

"I," said the old man, thinking hard, "am going to battle."

"Alone?" laughed Annikki, "and unarmed?"

"All right," said Väinämöinen, running out of ideas. "I'll tell you where I'm going—if you'll come into my boat with me!" That way, he thought, she will not be able to tell her brother.

"I'm sure," said Annikki, "that I'd bring you bad luck. I'm such a poor sailor. Even so," she added as sweetly as she knew how, "won't you please tell poor little Annikki where you're going?"

Väinämöinen could not resist any longer. "I'm going to the North Land," he said at last.

Annikki did not so much as stay to rinse out her washing. She jumped up and ran to the smithy, where her brother was busy at work among smoke and noise.

"Ilmarinen!" she shouted until he heard her and stopped. "I think your sister deserves a present for what she has to tell you. A ring, perhaps, or some earrings."

"If the news is important enough," her brother answered, "I'll make you all the jewelry you want. What is it?"

"Ilmarinen, do you still want to marry the Maid of the North?" And before he could say anything she went on, "While you're calmly working here somebody is

79

beating you to it. That crafty old Väinämöinen has just gone by in a boat—on his way to the North Land."

Ilmarinen paused a moment and said, "Annikki, get a bath ready for me. I'm going on a journey. And while you're lighting the fire I'll make you a few rings, and two or three pairs of earrings to match—or anything else you wish."

Annikki, in high spirits, gathered firewood and birch twigs, and hurried to the bath house with them. In a Finnish bath house—a *sauna*—you stand or sit on planks slung across a bed of stones, beneath which is a fire. Annikki laid and lit the fire, and when the stones were glowing hot she called her brother. She gave him a handful of birch twigs together with some soap she had prepared. While she was trying on her new jewels in front of her mirror, Ilmarinen was in the bath house, pouring water over the stones and standing in the hissing steam. He used the springy birch twigs to beat the dirt and grime out of his skin, and he was soon fresh and clean again.

There is really no need to explain this to Finnish children, for the Finns of today still enjoy their *sauna*—their steam bath—just as Ilmarinen did long ago. He took a towel and briskly rubbed the steam and perspiration from his body and out of his fair hair. Then he put on his best clothes—fine trousers and stockings, boots of strong German leather, a linen shirt, a blue coat lined with red, a warm woolen overcoat and a cape of the best fur over that, a belt adorned with gold and a gay pair of gloves, and, to crown it all, a splendid fur hat.

Everybody in the house helped him to get ready. His sledge was harnessed in his swiftest horse, and some folk say he even had six cuckoos perched on the sledge rail to sing songs of good omen on the way. He called on Ukko to send down a new fall of snow so that his sledge would glide more smoothly, and off he went to find his bride, with his family wishing him joy and waving goodbye.

Thundering along the lakeshore he soon caught up with Väinämöinen in his boat. He loved his old friend, and did not want to quarrel with him, especially over a wife.

"Väinämöinen!" he called out to the bearded figure in the boat, "let us make a friendly agreement; that neither of us shall carry off the Maid without the other's knowledge, but that she shall choose between us, and then there will be no hard feelings."

A most sensible idea, thought Väinämöinen, in the circumstances. And forever the best of friends they continued their journey to the North Land side by side, the one rowing along the lake, the other gliding along the shore.

THE WEDDING

The dogs began to bark. Over the misty Land of the North rang their warning from the house gates of Louhi. Life was going gently on its way with the cleaning, the cooking, the baking of bread, the chopping of wood, and nobody took much notice.

Still the dogs barked, more loudly and more excitedly, till Louhi stopped what she was doing and looked outside. There in the distance were two figures, one in a boat on the lake, the other riding along the lakeshore in a sledge drawn by a restless horse, both coming slowly nearer.

"Who's this?" she said to her daughter, who had joined her. "We'd better see what they want. I know an old way of telling whether strangers come in peace or for war. Put some rowan logs on the fire, my girl; if the logs ooze blood, then the strangers are for war; but if they give off water, then the strangers are peaceful."

Mother and daughter went back into the house and the Maid of the North put the logs on the fire. They sizzled and spat, and small drops of moisture appeared on them, forced out of the wood by the heat.

"This isn't blood—thank goodness for that—but . . . but it isn't water either!" old Louhi declared, bending over the flames. She stretched out a finger and cautiously touched one of the spluttering logs.

"Unless I'm very much mistaken," she said, putting the tip of her finger on her tongue, "this is honey! But how is it possible?"

There was a very old woman sitting huddled in the corner of the room with a blanket wrapped around her. She stirred and said, "If the log oozes honey, then the strangers come for marriage."

Louhi wasted no time at all. She took her daughter by the arm and led her outside. She pointed to where the suitors were approaching.

"Which one is it to be?" she said briskly. "You can't marry both of them. The one in the boat, I can see now, is Väinämöinen. He will bring you the wisdom of old age, and I dare say he's got one or two things of value in that boat of his too. And the one in the sledge—yes—is Ilmarinen. He's young and hot headed, and I don't expect for a minute he's brought you anything. He's probably filled his sledge with a load of spell-stuff, which will soon disappear into thin air.

"Anyway, daughter," she continued, "I leave it to you to choose between them. Choose carefully, don't be swept off your feet by good looks, for good looks don't always make a good husband. And listen; when they arrive, you will bring them a tankard of mead brewed from the best honey. Give it first to the one you've chosen. If I were you," she added, giving her daughter a nudge, "I'd pick the old one. He's got the brains and the money."

Well, thought the Maid, I think I should like to get married after all, but not to an old man. "Mother," she said, "I don't care about brains and money. I'd much rather have a husband who's young and handsome; and besides, Ilmarinen isn't so stupid, he made you the Sampo, remember."

"I'm only thinking of you, my girl," said Louhi, "with all that washing. Just imagine, getting your lovely white hands all red and chapped with scrubbing a smith's apron and rubbing the soot out of his hair!"

"Oh, but I'd quickly lose patience with a tiresome old man."

"These young people!" said Louhi, shrugging her shoulders. "But I suppose it's your life, so it's up to you."

"Yes, Mother," said the Maid firmly, "it's up to me."

Väinämöinen managed to arrive a few minutes before his friend. He moored his boat hastily and ran into the house, where the Maid was waiting for her suitors.

"Fair Maid of the North," he said as politely as he could, "will you come home with me and be my wife?"

Instead of answering his question, the Maid asked him one, "And have you made the boat out of my loom?"

Väinämöinen thought quickly. "If . . . if you're speaking of boats, O Maid," he said, "I have a magnificent one down at the lakeside. It has just brought me all the way here, and it will weather all storms and tempests."

"Oh, I've no time for sailors!" said the Maid. "Always bragging about their boats, always wanting to go to sea, with never a thought for the folk back at home! No, Väinämöinen, I will not go home with you and be your wife."

The old man was just about to offer her everything he could think of when a noise made him turn around. The young man had come in.

Ilmarinen looked more handsome than ever in his fine clothes. When he took off his hat his hair glowed pure gold in the firelight, and the Maid suddenly found herself head over heels in love. She fetched the tankard of mead and shyly offered it to the newcomer; but Ilmarinen held up his hand, refusing to accept it.

"Never will I touch the drink you offer me," he declared, "until my true love, she I have so long pined for, has called me her own."

The Maid was still finding words for an answer when her mother broke in.

"Right, well that's that," she said. "Off you go, my girl, and get changed. And in the meantime," she said, turning to a bewildered Ilmarinen, "I've got a job for you, my lad. Not far from here you'll find the Field of Vipers; if you're going to marry my daughter you must go and plough it for me. I had a son once, he had only ploughed half of it when . . . when he was bitten."

Unable to say any more, Louhi hurried off to find some housework, leaving Ilmarinen alone. Alone? Yes, nobody had noticed Väinämöinen go down to his boat and row wearily along the lake homeward. He was too old to marry—he realized it now; but he was used to living on his own.

Ilmarinen was thinking black thoughts. One viper, with its poisonous fangs, is enough to kill a man, and here was Louhi asking him to plough a field where vipers gather in spring after hibernation! Did she want her future son-in-law to die, as her own son had died? Did she want her daughter to marry Väinämöinen instead of him? Ilmarinen was not usually one to ask himself questions; he preferred doing things, and there was a job to be done now. But how? That was the hardest question of all. He was determined to marry the Maid . . . perhaps, yes, perhaps the Maid herself could advise him. It was worth a try, heaven knows. He went to the room where he had seen her go and knocked timidly on the door.

"Who's there?" asked the voice he loved.

"Me—Ilmarinen."

There was a rustling of clothes and the slam of a drawer being closed hurriedly. The door opened.

"Come inside—quickly," whispered the Maid, shutting the door behind him. "What is it you want? Mother will be furious if she finds you here."

"I don't think your mother wants you to marry me," said Ilmarinen sadly.

Her dark eyes opened wide. "Why ever not?"

"She has just told me to go and plough the Field of Vipers. Look, my darling," he said, "I may be slow sometimes, but I'm not stupid—after all, I did make the Sampo. But I can't think of a way to plough a field full of poisonous snakes without . . . well, without being killed."

"Don't say that," the Maid pleaded. "Mother has strange ideas sometimes. I expect she told you I had a brother who was killed ploughing that field, perhaps she wants to make sure you'll be a good son-in-law— and husband," she added with a blush.

"Perhaps," said Ilmarinen, "and I'm only too glad to prove that I shall be—but how?"

"There is a way. Forge yourself a plough of gold and silver, and you'll be safe. Now go," said the Maid, open- ing the door for him, "before Mother sees you."

If the Maid knew a safe way to plough the Field of Vipers, why had she not told her brother? Ilmarinen wondered; but he was tired of asking himself questions which seemed to have no answer. He went out to the smithy near the house. Luckily he had some gold and silver with him; they were to have been a present for his bride—Louhi would have been surprised if she had known. It did not take the great smith long to forge a shining plough, together with a pair of strong iron shoes, a coat of mail and some iron gloves as hard as stone. Then he climbed into his sledge and set off.

The Field of Vipers was a terrifying sight. The whole

landscape before him seemed to be alive with twisting, writhing forms, their black backs glistening with pale yellow zigzags. Even with the Maid's words glowing in his heart he hesitated.

"Come along, Ilmarinen," he said to himself, "there's work to be done."

He stepped out of his sledge, lifted the plough down and thrust it forward into the hissing mass.

"O evil vipers!" he called, to encourage himself, "if you rise against me, may Ukko send down a rain of arrows to strike you!"

Never looking behind him he strode on, his iron shoes trampling the moving earth, his coat of mail proof to the hooked teeth, gripping the marvelous plough through his iron gloves. Across and across the field he went, back and forth, while the vipers shot up in front of him, their gaping mouths gleaming venom, only to fall cursing under the bright plough, cheated of their victim.

The last furrow was done and Ilmarinen surveyed his work. The land was ready for anyone's sowing, with the furrows deep and straight and the ridges between them crisp in the slanting light—like so many snakes, thought the smith, except that they were straight and still. He loaded the plough back on to his sledge and drove back to where his anxious bride was waiting.

"I've ploughed the Field of Vipers for you," he told her mother. "May I marry your daughter now?"

"Since you're so clever," said the old woman, "you

can do something else that needs doing. Go and capture the Great Black Bear, the Bear of Tuoni, and put a harness on the Great Wolf of Tuoni. Many have gone out to catch these beasts, but none has returned."

The Bear of Tuoni. The Wolf of Tuoni. Bears and wolves were bad enough in the land of the living; what would they be like in Tuonela, the land of the dead? Surely Louhi was wishing him harm this time. More puzzled than ever, he went to the Maid and asked her advice again.

"Perhaps Mother wants to see whether you're brave enough to face death for me," said the Maid.

"You know I am, my love," said Ilmarinen, "but I should be facing death if I hunted bears and wolves even in the land of the living. How can I catch the Bear and the Wolf of Tuoni and not be torn to pieces?"

"There is a way. Forge muzzles of iron to fit over their mouths, and they won't be able to bite you."

Ilmarinen made two great iron muzzles, found some ropes, and set out for Tuonela. As he approached the dark region a thought suddenly struck him; surely the beasts would hear him coming! Now how could he dull the sound of his tread? He recalled a song he had learned long ago, and looking up into the gloomy sky he sang it:

> "Misty daughter Terhenetär!
> In your sieve now sift some cloud-mist

softly sprinkle now some vapor
where the game I seek is running
that it may not hear my footsteps
that it may not flee before me!"

A blue haze dropped lightly over the dead land, thick enough to muffle footsteps but thin enough to see through.

Ilmarinen looked about him. What he had thought earlier was a large bush nearby was a great black bear—the Great Black Bear of Tuoni it must be, for he had never seen such a fearsome creature before. It was a huge, tangled heap of malice, with eager, jagged teeth and hard little eyes. Ilmarinen could just hear it snuffling as it caught his scent and lumbered vaguely toward him. He tied a rope to one of the muzzles and crept around behind it.

Holding the muzzle in both hands with the rope dangling, he leaped at it and flung his arms over its head. Before the bear could turn itself around he had snapped the muzzle over its snout and was tugging at the rope.

He dragged the growling bear behind him over to a clump of squat trees, where he thought he could hear something sniffing and whimpering in the undergrowth. He saw a flash of coarse black hair and a long red mouth dripping saliva. It was the Great Wolf of Tuoni—there were the eyes, two dreadful lanterns glowing in the shade.

90

He grasped the muzzle in one hand, holding on to the struggling bear with the other, and made a dive at the slinking animal. There was a crashing of dry twigs and an angry snarl and the wolf was caught, still growling through its clamped teeth.

Ilmarinen dragged both bear and wolf out of Tuonela, and across the plains to Louhi.

"There," he panted, "I've caught the Great Black Bear and the Great Wolf of Tuoni for you. Now let me marry your daughter."

Louhi looked him up and down as he stood before her, the bear and the wolf straining at the ends of the ropes he was holding. Perhaps he will do after all, she mused—but not yet.

"A cleverer young man than I thought," she said to him. "Very well, one thing more and my daughter is yours. Go this time to the River of Tuonela and catch the Great Pike that swims in its waters—and catch it without using a net or a line. If you can do that, you're the only man alive who can."

She had the bear and the wolf taken away and followed them, leaving Ilmarinen alone and quite dismayed. I just hope, he thought rather ungraciously, that the Maid is a good wife to me after this!

For the third time he went and knocked on her door. Yes, he decided when she showed him in, she will be a good wife, anything is worth doing for her.

"I must catch the Great Pike in the River of

Tuonela," Ilmarinen told her gloomily, "without using a net or a line. I can catch trout with my fingers, but pike—that's quite a different matter. And the Great Pike of Tuonela as well! Oh, my love, what am I to do?"

"This is too much!" the Maid protested. "Nobody can do such a thing; but then," she pointed out, looking straight into his eyes, "nobody could plough the Field of Vipers, or capture the Bear and the Wolf of Tuoni, before you came along. Now, there's only one way I know to catch the Great Pike. You must use all your skill and forge an eagle—an eagle of living flame from your fire. The eagle will catch the pike for you, and you'll have no need of net or line. Good luck . . . my darling," she said shyly, squeezing his hand.

Ilmarinen went to the smithy, and stoked the fire into such a roaring blaze as the North Land had not seen since the Sampo was made. Deftly he caressed the sheets of flame into the form of a gigantic eagle, which he fitted with powerful claws of iron. Then he climbed on to the eagle's shoulders, singing:

> *"O my firebird, O my eagle!*
> *Go and fly where I shall bid you—*
> *down to Tuoni's murky river*
> *down to Manala's low regions!*
> *Strike the Pike, the huge and scaly*
> *that fine fish in waters darting!"*

The eagle flapped its wings of flame and soared brilliant into the sky, carrying a breathless Ilmarinen once more to the regions of the dead. Over the misty land it streaked, like a comet in the clouds, until it reached Tuonela, where it wheeled around and down and dropped to rest in the cavern of the river. Ilmarinen jumped off its shoulders on to the bank and scanned the dark waters, while the eagle stood by watching him.

Suddenly a wicked water spirit sprang out at Ilmarinen and tried to drag him into the swirling river. An unspeakable thing it was, which no man had ever seen and lived to describe. Before Ilmarinen knew what was holding him the eagle had seized it in its iron claws, twisted its neck and hurled it screaming back into the water, where it sank out of sight.

Now a wide ripple spread across the river, lapping both banks. Just below the surface Ilmarinen could make out the shape of a giant fish with two rows of pointed teeth on either jaw; from where he was standing it seemed to be nearly all mouth. This was the Great Pike of Tuonela, and it was coming straight for him, its blank eyes staring at him through the water.

The eagle flared up and rushed at the pike. Instead of scurrying away the pike broke the surface and grabbed one of the eagle's legs, trying to pull it into the water; but the eagle swung upward, taking the pike with it into the air.

The bird of flame hovered a moment, with the fish dangling from it by its teeth. Then it drove an iron claw into the pike's back and stretched out another claw to grip a rock; but the other claw slipped on the smooth rock, and the pike, seeing the eagle off balance, un-clenched its teeth, struggled loose and plunged back into the river, its scaly back bleeding from a deep wound.

The eagle soon righted itself and swooped on the pike again as it floundered in agony. This time both claws dug into the fish's back and the bird swept upward again with its prey secure and gasping; but instead of taking it back to Ilmarinen the eagle scorched past him through the dark air of the cavern and out to a tall tree. It settled on a high branch well out of its maker's reach and tore the pike fin from fin, ripping open its stained and glistening belly, wrenching away its breast-bone and hacking its cruel head from its body.

With a shout Ilmarinen dashed out to the tree and shook his fist up at the eagle as it smouldered far above him. The eagle dropped the pike's head down to him, and, carrying the rest of the fish with it, roared off into the clouds and was never seen again.

At least, thought Ilmarinen gloomily as he trudged back to Louhi, the head proves that the Great Pike of Tuonela has been caught.

"I've done what I could," he said, giving the head to Louhi. "Look, I've ploughed the Field of Vipers for you, I've captured the Bear and the Wolf of Tuoni, and I've caught the Great Pike of Tuonela without using a net or a line. Surely I can marry your daughter now?"

"Not so well done as I'd hoped," said Louhi, hard to

please. "It's my guess that you've made a meal of the pike's body, and brought me only the part you couldn't eat!"

Ilmarinen took a deep breath. "Mistress Louhi," he said patiently, "no one can expect to have the best catch without some sign of the trouble it took to get it. Besides, this fish was caught in the River of Tuonela. Now, where is my bride? Is she ready at last?"

"Yes, she's ready," said Louhi, her old face creasing into a smile. "I know too well," she went on a little sadly, "that a mother can't hope to have a beautiful daughter all to herself for always; she'll want to marry and make a home of her own. Maybe I have been rather stern with you, Ilmarinen, but I see now that you're a good boy. You'll take care of her, won't you?"

"I promise," said Ilmarinen.

"Good," said the old woman, brisk once more. "Well, if you'll excuse me, I must get on. There's a lot to be done, with a wedding in the family!"

And she bustled away, rolling up her sleeves and handing out orders to anybody she saw standing idle.

The North Land had never known such a wedding. To provide meat for the banquet a great ox was slaughtered. Some folk say that it was only a middle-sized one, but that even so it took a swallow a whole day to fly from the tip of one horn to the other, and a squirrel might scamper down its back for a month and not reach its tail.

Then a great hall was built in which to hold the banquet—so great, some say, that if a cockerel crowed at the smoke hole in the roof it would not be heard from the floor below, and if a dog barked at one end of it the sound would not reach the other end.

Louhi paced up and down the great hall, looking rather worried. "I've got somewhere to put them all," she was saying to herself, "and plenty of meat to feed them; but what shall I give them to drink? I'm no hand at brewing beer, and that's a fact."

"Perhaps I can help." An old man who was already sitting by the stove had overheard her. "I know the origin of beer," he said, "it's made from barley, flavored with hops, and brewed in water over a fire. Listen." And the old man told Louhi how beer was first made.

Long ago there was a tiny seed whose name was Hop. It was the son of Merriment, and it lived in good rich soil near a spring in Kalevala. One day, bored with doing nothing in the darkness, it pushed some green shoots up into the light and looked around. Towering above it was a tree, its leaves basking in the sun. If I can climb this tree, Hop thought, I shall have more sunshine than I get down here in the field; so up the tree trunk it went, its shoots growing fingers to cling as it climbed.

Another seed, called Barley, began pushing up its hairy shoots in the field below. One day Hop looked

96

down from its tree and saw Barley; and Barley looked up and saw Hop. "Oh who will introduce us?" they cried. "Life is so lonely here, up in the tree and down in the field, how we long for each other's company!"

It chanced that a young woman was passing by at the time, and she heard them. Her name was Osmotar, for she was the first girl to have been born in Osmola, or Kalevala, as most people call that land. She cut Barley from the field, plucked Hop from the tree and put them together in a large cauldron. Next, she poured water over them and lit a fire under them. Hop and Barley hummed happily as they brewed; and when the mixture was ready Osmotar poured it off into barrels to cool.

"And that," the old man concluded, "is how beer is made. It's a fine drink which warms a man and cheers a woman, but too much of it makes one mad."

Louhi thanked the old man for the recipe and set about brewing some beer herself. When she had done and while the brew was cooling in barrels, she put dozens of kettles on to boil. Mouth-watering smells stole out over the North Land as saucepans sizzled and puffed, bread baked and hundreds of pots of porridge bubbled and steamed.

Louhi forgot nothing. "When my guests have eaten and drunk their fill," she said to herself, "they'll want to be entertained. I must find a singer who knows the best songs, and who will perhaps sing the praises of the hostess too."

She sent men out to look for such a singer. They came back first with a salmon, for, they said, it had a wide mouth, fit surely for the greatest songs. But who ever heard of a fish singing? A wide mouth it might have, but its jaws were crooked. Next the men returned with a small boy, for, they said, he had a shrill voice, which would carry well. But the boy's tongue was not long enough to utter the longest words.

The men were about to continue their search for a singer when everybody heard a low, grumbling noise. It was coming from the barrels in which Louhi had stored the beer.

"If you don't find a singer soon," the noise seemed to be saying, "I'll burst out of these barrels and spill on the ground!"

Those men were stupid, Louhi thought; she called for some messengers. "Hurry, hurry," she commanded, "the beer is growing impatient. Go and invite the guests—all the poor people, all the blind and all the lame. Row the blind here in boats, bring the lame on horseback and in sledges. Invite all the folks of the North Land, and all the folks of Kalevala as well. And don't forget the great Väinämöinen, for he, he is to be my singer!"

The messengers ran off on their errands and Louhi busied herself outside the house for a while. She looked up from her work and saw a vast crowd of people approaching across the snow.

"Oh dear . . . oh dear!" she muttered. "What's this?

I hope I'm not going to be invaded—it looks like an army!"

She need not have worried, though. A few minutes later she recognized Ilmarinen in the crowd; he had been home and was bringing all his relatives to the wedding.

The day came, and everything was ready just in time. Louhi had hardly slept over the last few days with worrying about it all. She had even been fretting in case the doorway leading into the great hall were not high enough for the bridegroom to walk through without knocking his head! Everywhere was spick and span, the walls and floors had been scrubbed, the windows cleaned and polished till they winked in the sun.

Gradually the guests arrived and trooped in their thousands into the hall. Ilmarinen was treated with the highest honor. All the small boys of the North Land went to greet their hero; they removed his hat and gloves politely, and led his horse gently away to the most comfortable stable and the tastiest oats. They showed him into the hall and up past the cheering guests to the top table, where his bride and her mother received him.

The Maid of the North had never looked so lovely before, in her richly embroidered red, yellow and blue wedding-dress, her dark hair resplendent with jewels and ribbons, and her dark eyes dancing with the greatest happiness she had ever known. Ilmarinen sat down beside her, his heart full of joy and love; and the wedding feast began.

First there were cream cakes, served with butter, to give everyone a good appetite. Then came the dish which Finns enjoy to this day—the finest fish with the whitest pork, eaten together. This is a very rich dish which keeps out the cold; and there is plenty of cold to keep out in Finland.

Fish and meat were piled high on every plate—there was scarcely room at the edge to put the bones. The great ox was brought in and carved; there was salmon, there was bread, still warm from the ovens, and there were steaming bowls of porridge for all who wanted them.

Now it was time for the beer. The barrels were tapped and the beer gushed foaming and sparkling into a thousand tankards. When everybody had eaten and drunk enough—well, enough for the time being—Väinämöinen, the great, aged singer, rose to his feet.

"Friends," he began, "I am old, and my voice is not what it was. Is there nobody here who will sing the old stories to us and praise Mistress Louhi for the noble feast she has set before us?"

There was a general groan of disappointment that Väinämöinen might not be singing after all, and a boy stood up and offered to entertain the guests.

"Only the old and wise know the best songs," spoke up an old man somewhere in the hall. "The voices of children are sweet, but they are not strong. Let the oldest and wisest among us be our singer."

All the guests agreed, including the boy who had stood up, and they agreed too that Väinämöinen was not only the oldest and wisest, but the greatest singer as well. He alone, they said, was worthy to sing. So Väinämöinen, who had loved and lost the Maid of the North, sang at her wedding; and if his voice quavered a little as he sang, perhaps it was because he was so old.

Afterward, just as at all weddings, there were speeches. People stood up and told the bride she was a married woman now and being married meant washing and cleaning and cooking—all very sound advice, no doubt, but it took so long! Then it was the bridegroom's turn; Ilmarinen was told to take good care of his wife, always to be loving and kind to her and never to let her work too hard.

All the excitement proved too much for the Maid, and she burst into tears. The speeches were over by now and she noticed with alarm that everyone was looking at her! She bravely dried her eyes and stood up.

"Dear friends," she said in a voice which was clear, even if it was a bit unsteady, "the time is coming for us all to return home. You will go to your old homes, but I shall be going to a new one—with my husband. Although I am leaving the North Land, a part of me will always remain behind on my good mother's farm. Out on the far border of our farthest field is a hedge; I laid that hedge out myself, when I was a little girl. If anyone should call here looking for me, that is all they will find of me, for I belong with Ilmarinen from this day onward. Farewell, dear friends, and thank you all for your good wishes."

Ilmarinen's horse and sledge were waiting outside. He lifted the Maid into it, and with everybody waving and cheering they set out across the snow on the long journey to Kalevala. The Maid could not help feeling sad as the house in which she had grown up disappeared from view. As the northern sun sank lower Ilmarinen wrapped another rug around her shoulders and she snuggled up beside him. No, she decided, she would not be anywhere else, not for anything in the world.

The sledge glided into the darkness.

lmarinen, "let's go off to the North Land and capture the Sampo."

"But, Väinämöinen," said the smith, putting down his hammer, "I made it for Louhi and it's hers. Anyway," he added, "she's my mother-in-law."

"I know all that," said the old man impatiently. "Listen, haven't we had a bad harvest? Isn't life hard for us these days? Can't you see this fair land of ours going to rack and ruin? Meanwhile the North Land is flourishing and growing richer and richer—thanks to the Sampo which you made. I think it's high time we had a turn with it, to help us out of our troubles."

Sometimes Ilmarinen could not follow his friend's arguments, and this was one of those times; but he always thought it was because he was slow witted, so he agreed.

"But, Väinämöinen," he said again, "the Sampo is locked away inside the Copper Mountain behind nine great locks and fastened down with three mighty roots."

Väinämöinen was not one to be put off by mere mountains. "That's no problem," he said, though it was —but he would think of something as he always did. "All we need is a boat big enough to carry it off in, and it's as good as ours."

Ilmarinen was not at all happy with the idea. Louhi

was a pleasant old woman, provided that—and only provided that—you were her friend. "Couldn't we . . . couldn't we ask her for it?" he suggested lamely. "Anyway, I'm no sailor. A sledge is far safer than a boat. If you meet a storm on land you can always take shelter; but if you were to meet one on the water you might sink, and then where would you be?"

"Well, yes," Väinämöinen replied, stroking his beard. "Traveling by land is safer, I grant you, but it's so tiring. Just think of the joys of sailing, gliding over the lakes, swaying gently in the wind with not a care in the world! However, my friend, if you'd really prefer to go by land, then we will."

Ilmarinen had hoped perhaps that Väinämöinen would not want to go, if he could not go by boat; but there it was, they were going and that was that.

"First," Väinämöinen went on, "you must make me a new sword, long enough, strong enough and sharp enough to cut through a mountain."

Ilmarinen stoked up his fire and heated some iron till it was as soft as soup. Then he beat it on his anvil into the most marvelous sword even he had ever seen; its blade glinted with both the sun and the moon at once. As soon as it was cool Väinämöinen took it away to try on a mountain; one swish of the sword and the mountain crumbled into ten thousand rocks.

When Väinämöinen returned Ilmarinen was already preparing the horse and sledge for the journey. A few moments and they were passing along a lakeshore on their way.

"What's that noise?" asked Ilmarinen suddenly. "It seems to be coming from those reeds."

"Sounds like somebody weeping," said Väinämöinen, cupping a hand to his ear. "A girl, maybe. Let's go down and see."

A large boat was moored among the reeds at the lakeside. Whoever was weeping seemed to be in the boat. More curious than ever, the two heroes leaned over the reed-bed and looked down into the boat. Not a soul in sight—man, woman or child. On and on went the weeping, louder and more distressed.

The men looked at each other. They had the same idea at the same time. Surely . . . surely it was not the boat itself weeping! Who ever heard of a boat weeping? Ilmarinen began to feel uneasy. He gave Väinämöinen a nod, which meant, "You speak to it. I wouldn't know what to say."

"What is it, good boat?" asked the old man gently— he had a way with boats. "Don't tell me that such a fine specimen of boathood has been declared unseaworthy!"

"Oh no, it's nothing like that," said the boat between sobs. "Can you imagine how a girl feels if she can't find a husband? That's how I feel, stuck here among these reeds instead of speeding through the water with the wind in my sails. When I was built they told me I was to be a warship, going on exciting voyages to distant lands, but I've had precious little in the way of adventure so far. And what makes me so wild is that there are plenty of boats, not nearly as beautiful as I, having the time of their lives on the high seas, while I just sit here watching the world go by, with frogs and toads jumping and crawling all over me—ugh! How I wish I were still a tree; at least I'd have squirrels for company, instead of these slimy creatures!" And the boat burst into tears again.

"There, there," said Väinämöinen soothingly. "I expect you feel better now you've got all that off your . . . your chest. Well, boat, I've good news for you. As a warship you were built, and a warship you shall be. It so happens that my friend here"—he pointed to a bemused Ilmarinen—"and I am going to war this very day; so let's not waste any more time—eh, Ilmarinen?"

The boat's sobs stopped abruptly, and the water lapping its sides sounded like the clapping of hands. Ilmarinen was still trying to puzzle out what had happened as Väinämöinen, with a twinkle in his eye, tied their horse to a tree where there was plenty of green grass, and helped him rather unsteadily down into the boat. A quick song to get things going and the boat was out on the open lake.

But still it was not happy. It tossed about impatiently and Väinämöinen was beginning to wonder whether it was such a good boat after all.

"Boat," he called to the timbers he was sitting on,

"are you sure you're as good as you look?"

"I certainly am," replied the boat haughtily, "but what sort of a navy is two men, may I ask? Need I say there's room for quite a few more on board me."

Indeed, thought Väinämöinen, a few more hands would come in useful, both on deck and under a mountain. He cleared his throat and began singing. Nobody knows where they came from, but in minutes the boat was riding the waves superbly, its sides well nigh bursting with handsome young men, their hair neatly brushed, their boots shining, beautiful girls with jewels in their hair, girdles of glowing copper and their fingers sparkling with rings, and some old folk who might enjoy the trip, to fill in the odd corners.

"Action stations, lads," Väinämöinen called to the young men as he sat down at the tiller, "take the oars and row for all you're worth. We're bound for the North Land."

The young men took the oars, but heave and groan as they might they could not shift the boat so much as from one wave to the next.

"Some fine strapping lasses we have here," said Väinämöinen, resourceful as ever. "Come along girls, let's see whether you're stronger than the boys."

The girls seized the oars from the young men, but the boat might just as well have been at anchor.

"Business before pleasure, my friends," said Väinämöinen to the old folk; "I'm sure you'll enjoy the trip so much more if you take your share of the work. Come now, let's see the old ones set an example to the youngsters."

The old folk wrapped their skinny fingers around the oars and tugged, but the boat went backward if it moved at all.

"Here, let me have a go," said Ilmarinen, glad of a job to do. He took a pair of oars in his huge and powerful hands, and with a jerk the boat was under way. The water splashed, the timbers creaked, the oars cried out as the prow dipped and rose like a swan and the forests sped past on either side.

Whose boat was this in such a hurry and with such a crowd on board? a tall young man wondered as he gazed down the lake from his island. Life was hard these days for Lemminkäinen too. His crops had failed, and even his fishing was not what it might be.

"Ahoy there!" he bellowed. "Who comes this way?"

"Can't you see for yourself?" the young men in the boat bellowed back.

"Ah, now I can. Why, it's my old friend Väinämöinen—and Ilmarinen! Where are you bound for, my hearties?"

"We're heading for the North Land," Väinämöinen called, "to carry off the Sampo."

"Pull in and take me with you," called Lemminkäinen. "I'm quite handy with a sword, you know."

So they pulled in to the island and Lemminkäinen

strode aboard, carrying a bundle of planks on his shoulder.

"Why the planks?" asked Väinämöinen, greeting him. "We've plenty of timber on board, and besides we're pretty well loaded as it is."

"The prop never knocked the haystack over," said Lemminkäinen. "You can never have too much timber when you're going north. Those storms can knock a boat about a tidy bit."

They pulled out once more into the center of the lake and continued gaily on their way, their songs floating out across the water and echoing through the gloomy forests. After a while they noticed they were gathering speed, although Ilmarinen was still rowing at the same stout pace. Lemminkäinen knew what this meant, they were approaching a waterfall—fast. Since his narrow escape from the River of Tuonela his mother had taught him some water songs, in case he was ever in similar trouble again. He remembered the Song of Waterfalls, and began singing it just in time:

"Leave off, waterfall, your foaming
mighty water, cease your rushing!
Daughter of the foaming rapid
sit you on the dripping boulder
on the trickling rock O sit you!
Stem with your embrace the billows
with your hands wrap them together

gather in your fist their foaming
that they may not splash our bosoms
nor upon our heads may shower! . . ."

Lemminkäinen sang as Väinämöinen carefully steered the boat over the precipice, down the roaring wall of water, through the rocks and the blinding spray, and out into another calm lake. Everybody was cheering the skill of singer and helmsman, when suddenly the boat grated to a stop in the middle of the lake.

"Lemminkäinen, Lover-Man," said Väinämöinen, "look overboard and see what's holding us. We may have run aground, or tangled in some fallen branches."

The young man looked. "Well, would you believe it?" he said. "It's not a rock, it's not branches, it's not even a wreck. We're sitting on a fish, a pike—the largest pike I've ever seen."

"I'm not surprised," said Väinämöinen coolly. "You find all sorts of things in lakes. Give it a stab with your sword."

Lemminkäinen drew his sword and lunged at the pike so hard that he tumbled overboard with a yell and a splash.

"Steady on!" cried Ilmarinen. "Not so clever as we thought, eh?" he said as he hauled him back into the boat. "Let me try."

Ilmarinen drew his sword and dealt the pike such a blow that his sword snapped in pieces, and the fish was not even scratched.

"Not so clever either, then!" said Väinämöinen. "And now let me show you two gentlemen how the job is really done."

Väinämöinen drew his new sword and drove it hard and straight down through the pike's shoulders. Then he dragged the pike on his sword out from beneath the boat, up through the air, and flung it down with a thud into the boat.

Now that the boat was free to move again he steered it to a shore and ran it up on the sand.

"Time for dinner and a rest before we go on," he announced, and proceeded to cut up the pike for cooking. It was so large that it fed the whole company till they were quite full. Only one thing more is needed, thought Väinämöinen, and that is some music to help our digestion. He looked contentedly about him and his gaze settled on the huge piles of fishbones lying everywhere. Mm, I wonder, he thought.

"What," he said with a yawn, "can be made out of fishbones?"

"Nothing," said Ilmarinen, "nothing at all. Even the most skillful craftsman can make nothing out of fishbones. They're quite useless."

"On the contrary," said Väinämöinen, raising a sleepy hand. "I think a *kantele* could be made out of fishbones. Is anybody here clever enough to make a *kantele* of fishbones?"

Apparently there was nobody. In fact, some of the folk were probably thinking the old fellow was beginning to lose that wisdom he was so famous for. But then, as they all watched, Väinämöinen picked up the giant pike's jawbone, and, using its teeth as pegs, wound a hair from one tooth across the jawbone to the tooth opposite. He took another hair and wound that across from tooth to tooth, and another, and another, until there were five hairs strung taut across the white jawbone. The oldest kind of *kantele* has five strings, and here was a beautiful white *kantele*, fashioned from fishbones.

"Where did you get the hairs from, Väinämöinen?" asked one of the young men.

"From the tail of the Devil's Horse," replied the old man mysteriously, and the young man had to be content with that.

"Can anybody here play my fishbone *kantele*?" asked Väinämöinen, holding up the wonderful instrument. Several people tried—young men, girls, old folk, but not a single note did the *kantele* sing.

"Give it to me," said Lemminkäinen. "I'm sure I can get a tune out of it with my water-wisdom." Lemminkäinen drew his fingers across the strings, and the sound made everybody laugh; it was more the sound of a horse than of a *kantele*.

Väinämöinen took the *kantele* himself, and to everybody's delight caressed from it the most beautiful music they had ever heard. All the animals in the forests pricked up their ears and came running, hopping and lolloping to where Väinämöinen was sitting. Squirrels and deer, bears and wolves, all forgot their fear and fury as the *kantele* sang beneath the old man's fingers. Far away in Tapiola they heard it too and listened. All the birds, from the eagle and the swan to the humblest sparrow, cocked their heads to one side as they hovered in the air or sat on nearby branches. The Daughters of Creation, Kuutar the moondaughter, Päivätär the daughter of day, stopped combing the woolly clouds and spinning the rainbow for a moment. Even the fish—pike, salmon, perch, roach and the rest swam entranced to the lake shore. And Mother Nature herself, Väinämöinen's own ageless mother, paused and listened proudly to her greatest son.

Tears flowed freely that day—tears of joy at the music of the white *kantele*. And as he played Väinämöinen wept with the world he had charmed. Marvelous tears he wept, marvelous as the music that was calling them forth, for they became priceless blue pearls.

The North Land? The Sampo? For a while such thoughts were as far away as the stars.

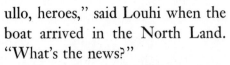

ullo, heroes," said Louhi when the boat arrived in the North Land. "What's the news?"

"The Sampo," said Väinämöinen curtly. "We've come to share it with you."

Ilmarinen groaned to himself. This was not the way to go about things. He was not surprised when Louhi replied to Väinämöinen, "I have no wish to . . . to saw my Sampo in half. It's doing quite well for itself inside its mountain, thank you, and there it will stay—every bit of it. Life is going smoothly for us now, and we in the North Land intend to keep it so."

"If you won't give back to us half of what we've given you," said Väinämöinen indignantly, "we'll take all of it by force and carry it off in our boat!" And he stormed away.

This means war, thought Louhi. She was not going to give up her Sampo without a fight. She warned the men of the North Land and told them to prepare their weapons.

Meanwhile Väinämöinen had taken up his fishbone *kantele* and begun to play it. All over the North Land people heard the music, amazed. They stopped whatever they were doing and sat down to listen, laughing with delight and weeping with joy; and before long they were all fast asleep, lulled by the marvelous sounds.

As soon as Väinämöinen heard the even breathing,

the snores and the whistles coming from everywhere, he laid his *kantele* aside, put his hand into his pocket and pulled out his purse. Purses are usually for holding money, of course, but Väinämöinen's purse contained two tiny needles. In a remarkably short time he had knitted together the lashes of every eye in the slumbering North Land, so that even if people did wake they could not see what the heroes were doing.

What were they doing? They were running out to the Copper Mountain, where the Sampo was locked away behind its nine locks and rooted down with its three roots. Once again Väinämöinen began singing, this time it was a song for making mountains tremble. While he sang, Ilmarinen and the young men smeared butter on the locks and bolts of the mountain's great door, and they rubbed bacon fat on the hinges, so that there would be no noise when the door was opened. As it turned out, hardly any sword-work was needed, for with only a little persuasion the mountain door swung clear, and the heroes stood gazing in wonder at the Sampo.

"Well, what are we waiting for?" said Väinämöinen impatiently. "Lemminkäinen, you look the biggest, go inside and bring it out here."

"I dare say I could do that without straining myself, man of muscle that I am," said Lemminkäinen, never short of a word in praise of himself; and he bounded into the cave.

While the others watched, Lemminkäinen put a

shoulder to the Sampo and pushed. Nothing happened. He put his other shoulder to it and pushed. Still nothing happened. He stretched his arms out sideways and heaved with his hands and his chest. Then he went down on all fours and tried to shift it from underneath—but the Sampo refused to budge as much as a finger-breadth.

The heroes had burst open the nine locks, but they could not tear up the three roots, by which the Sampo was fixed to the floor of the cave.

It was just as well, you might say, that there was an enormous bull in a meadow not far from the mountain. Uncommonly helpful for a bull, it let itself be led to the cave and harnessed to a plough. As the bull tugged and snorted, the plough churned the roots of the Sampo up out of the mountain's floor, and the precious object was free. It was hoisted on to many shoulders and borne swiftly down to where the boat was waiting, while the bull, no doubt, wandered off, wondering what all the fuss was about.

An hour, perhaps two hours passed, the only sound being the splash and creak of oars as the boat sped southward with its fabulous cargo. Then Lemminkäinen, who could never be quiet for long, said, "Where are all our voices? Here we are, sailing home with our Sampo at last, and we're not singing!"

"There's a time and a place for singing," said Väinämöinen wisely, "and it's not here, or now. Singing will slow us up and bring the darkness too soon."

Väinämöinen was right; there would be darkness, darkness over the whole world—but not for some time yet. And all due, perhaps, to what followed.

"Look," said Lemminkäinen, pointing to the west, "the sun is sinking anyway. I really don't see how a song will make it sink faster."

Silence. A little more time passed, then, "Why not sing? We've got the Sampo and we're well on our way now. Come on, Väinämöinen, give us a song!" Lemminkäinen was obstinate.

"I'll tell you why not," said Väinämöinen. "It's still too early to sing. Let's get home first, and we'll have something to sing about."

"If you won't sing, old man," said Lemminkäinen almost angrily, "then I will!" He opened his mouth, and out came the most dreadful wailing sound. All around the sky the noise he called singing echoed and rang.

Far away, standing one legged on a rock in the middle of a swamp, a crane was counting its toes and minding its own business as cranes do. When it heard Lemminkäinen's yelling it was scared out of its tiny wits, and let out a scream of terror. Forgetting its curious pastime the crane swung up from its rock into the air and flew off, straight over the North Land, screaming and yawping all the way.

The people of the North Land stirred in their blissful slumbers and woke with a start as the terrified crane passed overhead. There was a furious unpicking of eyelashes as everybody, including old Louhi herself, wondered what had happened. Louhi ran out into her farmyard to see whether anything was missing. The corn was still standing where it had been stacked to dry in the fields; the cattle were still all there in the meadow, chewing the cud and looking as bored as ever. Louhi made a quick guess, and hurried away to the Copper Mountain, where she kept the . . .

It was gone! The doors of the mountain were open and swinging back and forth on their hinges, and the cave was empty. Now who . . . ? The question was not worth asking. Trembling with rage, Louhi called upon the spirit who had helped Ilmarinen in happier days:

> *"Misty daughter, girl of vapor!*
> *In your sieve not sift some cloud-mist*
> *softly sprinkle now some vapor*
> *let the clouds down from the heavens*
> *and a haze out of the weather*
> *down upon the lake's clear surface*
> *out upon the open water*
> *to confound old Väinämöinen*
> *and for him to lose his bearings! . . ."*

Next Louhi called on Iku-Turso—Turso the Everlasting, a strange and terrible sea beast, to rise out of the lake, sink Väinämöinen's boat and return the Sampo to her; and finally she called on Ukko himself, to send a storm. This is the best kind of spell, by the way, for getting things done; you call first on the little spirits who are nearest to hand; then, in case they cannot help, you call on the greater and more powerful spirits—sea beasts and the like; and finally, in case *they* cannot help, you call on Ukko, who can always step in if necessary—and your spell is complete. It would, of course, be bad manners to call on Ukko first; he would not appreciate being asked to do a job which a mere local spirit could manage with ease; he has enough to think about as it is, being Chief Spirit and Lord of the Weather.

The boat went on its way with Ilmarinen rowing, Lemminkäinen singing, and Väinämöinen feeling sure that something would happen before they all reached home.

Suddenly a mist came down all around the boat, so thick that they could hardly see one another. Ilmarinen stopped rowing. There was no point in continuing, he thought; for all you knew you might row yourself back to the North Land or straight into a forest. We must simply wait for the mist to clear, he thought.

Väinämöinen thought differently. "Are we going to let a mist hold us up?" he said. He drew his sword, raised it in the air and plunged it into the lake; and, as suddenly as the mist had come down, it lifted and disappeared. Väinämöinen was cleverer than the girl of vapor.

Ilmarinen took up the oars again and was just about to row, when the water on one side of the boat started bubbling and swirling as though it were coming to a boil. Ilmarinen turned quite pale and pulled his cap down over his eyes—he had always said he would rather travel by land. But Väinämöinen looked down into the lake to see what was causing the disturbance.

"So it's you, Iku-Turso!" he cried, hauling the wretched beast out of the water by its ears. "And what do you think you're doing, giving us all such a fright?"

Nobody had ever spoken to Iku-Turso like this before, and he was quite startled.

"Come along!" said Väinämöinen, shaking him, "answer me, what's the meaning of it?"

"I . . . it was Louhi," stammered Iku-Turso, blinking his huge eyes. "She gave me orders to sink your boat and return the Sampo to her; but—oh!" he yelped as Väinämöinen yanked him to and fro, "if you'll let me go I'll never bother you again."

"So I should hope!" said Väinämöinen, releasing him; and from that day to this nobody has ever seen Iku-Turso. Väinämöinen was cleverer than the sea beast.

Ilmarinen pushed back his cap and took up the oars once more. No sooner had he done so than a howling noise came from the west; then a howling, rushing noise came from the south; then a rushing, roaring noise from the east; from the north too came the wind, tearing through the forests, stripping the trees of their leaves and whipping the waters into a foaming, seething fury.

The heroes clung to the boat for their lives. Väinä-

THE BATTLE

möinen's beautiful white *kantele* of fishbones was swept
overboard and lost for ever. Ilmarinen, who had always
said he was no sailor, was quite ill and kept shouting
"Help! Help!" until a wave splashed right into his open
mouth and made him sick again.

"Shouting for help will get us nowhere in the middle
of a lake," Väinämöinen pointed out, and he began
singing:

> *"Water, water, check your boy-child*
> *billow, billow, chide your offspring*
> *Ahto, Ahto, quell the rollers*
> *Vellamo, conquer the water*
> *that it may not splash the timbers*
> *may not reach above my boat-ribs!*
>
> *Wind, O wind, rise to the heavens*
> *up into the clouds go chase you*
> *to your kindred, to your country*
> *to your tribe and to your family!*
> *Do not spill this wooden vessel*
> *do not sink this boat of pinewood!*
> *Rather fell the trees in clearings*
> *and on hills blow down the spruces!"*

Lemminkäinen remembered his planks, and, as the
stormed calmed to Väinämöinen's song, he built up the
sides of the boat in case there was any more trouble. It
was just as well he did.

"Climb aloft to the masthead," said Väinämöinen,

when the lake was still again, "and see whether there are any clouds about."

Lemminkäinen did so. "All clear," he called down. "Wait a moment, though . . . yes, northward . . . northward I see one small cloud."

"Nonsense!" said Väinämöinen. "That's no cloud, that's a boat. Have another look."

Lemminkäinen wondered how the old man could possibly see better from below, but he had another look. "You're right, it's not a cloud. It's a . . . it's an island, I'm sure. I can see trees . . . and I can even see birds in the trees."

"Nonsense!" Väinämöinen repeated. "Birds in the trees—ha. Men in a boat, I'd say—and men of the North Land, at that."

"Oh dear, you're right too," said Lemminkäinen, sliding down the mast. "It's a large boat, full of warriors from the North Land—and it's coming this way. What shall we do?"

"Row!" answered Väinämöinen. "Row hard, everybody!" he told the young men and the girls and the old folk. The boat leaped forward, but, row as they might, they made little progress, the other boat was slowly gaining on them. Now what do we do? thought Väinämöinen, scratching his ancient head. An idea was not long in coming.

He opened his tinder box, and took out one of those small pieces of tree fungus which smolder when a spark falls on them. He scraped some pitch from between the planks of the boat, and threw it with the tinder over his shoulder into the lake, singing:

> *"Of this let a reef be fashioned*
> *made of this a secret island*
> *which the North Land's boat shall run on*
> *fitted with the hundred rowlocks*
> *dash against it in a tempest*
> *and amid the waves be shattered!"*

Still nearer came the other boat, so near that Väinä-möinen could see old Louhi herself jumping up and down and waving her arms in fury, when a wind sprang screaming from nowhere. The Northmen had their oars snatched out of their hands, and the boat pitched giddily out of control. In calmer water not far away, the heroes watched with glee as—C R U N C H ; the North Land's boat ran straight on to the rocks which had been Väinä-möinen's piece of tinder and tar.

Louhi and her men tumbled out on to the reef and pushed and pulled at their boat, trying to refloat it, but in vain. Besides, it was so badly damaged that it would have sunk. But Louhi soon had another plan.

As the storm subsided, she took a few of the scythes which her men had brought as weapons—these would do for claws; then around her she arranged parts of the shattered boat—the sides would make good wings and the rudder a tail.

"Climb up on my back!" she screeched to the men, for she had become a great eagle of wood and iron. She soared into the sky with her men, and swooped down on Väinämöinen's boat.

"Hullo, Louhi!" said Väinämöinen brightly as she settled on a sailyard, her enormous weight making the boat keel over dangerously. "Will you share the Sampo with us now?"

"No I will not!" screamed the old woman-eagle, and with her beak she tried to snatch the Sampo out of the boat. Lemminkäinen drew his sword and struck at her claws as she went to take off into the air again. Väinämöinen too seized an oar and beat her with it. The men of the North Land fell from her back into the water, like so many squirrels jumping down from a tree.

Louhi tried once more—with a finger this time, her third, nameless finger, the most powerful finger of all. She whisked the Sampo out of the boat, and before anyone knew what had happened she had flung it into the lake, where it smashed into pieces and most of the pieces sank to the bottom. And that, some folk say, is why the sea is so rich in fish and oysters and pearls and coral and all the thousand and one things that come from the sea; for since that day the Sampo has belonged to the kingdom of the waters.

Not all of the Sampo was lost, though; a few small pieces remained floating on the lake.

"Anyway," said Väinämöinen to Louhi as her men

climbed on her back again, "I can plant these pieces in the soil of Kalevala."

"You may do what you like with them," said Louhi with a grim laugh. "I will send you so many curses and ills that your land will soon be no more!"

"Threats from the North Land don't mean much to me," said Väinämöinen. "Try some of them out on yourself!"

With a screech of anguish Louhi wheeled into the air and flew homeward. All she had of the Sampo now was the smallest piece—that piece which had come off on her nameless finger. It was hard times once again for the North Land.

When Väinämöinen returned to Kalevala he sowed the fragments of the Sampo and called on Ukko to bless the land. Happiness at last, he thought; but the real troubles were only just beginning.

MOON, SUN & FIRE

A bird sang in Kalevala. Across golden fields where the corn was being harvested, through forests smiling in the summer sun, over sparkling lakes rang its song—cuckoo, cuckoo, it echoed. The bird of better days had arrived, and the fair land of the south was joyful and flourishing once more. Two men, however, were walking by a lakeside with faces full of sadness.

"Life is good in Kalevala," Väinämöinen was saying, "but how can I give voice to the happiness of my people —how, without my beloved *kantele* of fishbones? Ahto, the Lord of the Waters, has it now; I can hardly expect him to send it back to me. Ilmarinen," he went on, turning to his companion, "make me a rake, and I'll go out in a boat to look for it along the paths of the salmon."

The two men made their way to Ilmarinen's workshop, where once again the smith found himself beating out a long rake. He gave it to Väinämöinen, who sailed off to the lake where he had lost his *kantele*. When he judged, from the shape of the forests and the positions of the small islands, the place where it had been washed overboard in the storm, he stretched out his rake and dragged it backward and forward through the water. Leaves of water lilies, lumps of old wood, bits of rushes —the rake picked up everything, it seemed, but the white *kantele*. Sadder than ever Väinämöinen rowed home, moored his boat, and went for a walk in a forest.

He had not been walking very long when he heard a sound of weeping somewhere in front of him. He quickened his pace until he reached a silver birch tree, whose slender branches were trembling in the breeze. If boats could weep, then surely trees could as well.

"Beautiful silver birch," said Väinämöinen, "why are you so unhappy? Don't tell me you're anxious to go to war?"

"Oh no," wept the tree, "it's nothing like that. Just look at me, though, one silver birch surrounded by stupid willows, can you imagine how lonely I get? And another thing, people come along and chop off my branches, or carve their initials in my trunk, or peel off my silver bark. Then the wind comes and tears off my leaves; and when it's winter—oh!—I get so cold that I shake from crown to root."

"Poor tree," said Väinämöinen kindly, "don't be so distressed. You're a good supple birch, I can see, and from now on you'll sing for joy."

Supple? Well, I dare say I am as supple as the next birch, thought the tree, but what does the old man mean? A moment later it found out, as Väinämöinen, with sudden strength, bent it around into a curious shape and went off.

Some cuckoos were sitting in an oak tree, pouring out their song of gold and silver. Väinämöinen gathered up the gold and silver and shaped it into pegs, which he brought back to the birch tree and drove into its trunk and limbs. Väinämöinen went off again, and found a girl with long, golden hair, singing for her lover to come soon.

"But five fine hairs give me, O maiden," begged Väinämöinen, "and I will make them sing."

The girl had probably given away one or two locks of her hair before now, and here was an old man asking for five strands only! She thought she could give them away without feeling a draught. She pulled them out and handed them to him.

Back at the birch tree Väinämöinen wound each hair around a peg made of cuckoo song, and stretched it across to the peg on the opposite branch. Five hairs—five strings; and the birch tree *kantele* was ready for playing.

Väinämöinen reached out his fingers, and the tree forgot its sorrow and sang. Mountains, lakes and all the other trees listened to the new music. It is even said that some tree stumps stopped grieving at what they had lost, and hopped and jumped about in time to Väinämöinen's song. Throughout the land old women danced as though they were young again, and young girls dabbed their eyes with tiny handkerchiefs as they listened. All the animals in the forests sat up on their hind legs in order to hear better, birds crowded together on branches, fish in the silent lakes stopped chewing and swam to the shores, and even worms wriggled up out of the earth to listen to Väinämöinen as he played his tree.

From that day, onward, whenever Väinämöinen walked in the forest, all the trees would bow politely as he passed. Life was good for Väinämöinen too, now that he could give voice to the happiness of the people.

"Oho, so they're doing all right down there in Kalevala, are they? I'll soon put a stop to that." Eaten up with jealousy, Louhi kept the grim promise she had made that day of the battle on the lake. She sent the nine sons of a vile old woman from Tuonela, nine dreadful sicknesses to visit the happy land in the south.

It was an evil time for Kalevala then, as the people sickened and many died. Väinämöinen worked hard with songs and ointments night and day. He heated bath houses all over the ailing land, to bring comfort to his people; and he called on spirits to help him in the struggle against Tuonela, the kingdom of death:

> "... *Kivutar, pain's noble mistress*
> *Vammatar, hurt's choicest matron*
> *come along now, go along now*
> *to perform a work of healing*
> *and to work for peace among us!*
> *Treat the pains till they are painless*
> *hurts until they hurt no longer*
> *that the sick may sink in slumber*
> *that the weak may rest from worry*
> *and the one in pain be peaceful*
> *and the sufferer lie quiet!*

Put the pains into a barrel
hurts into a copper casket
and the pains far from us carry
and the hurts cast down far from us
in the midst of the Pain-Mountain
on the summit of the Pain-Hill!
There heat up the pains to boiling
in a tiny little kettle
one no bigger than a finger
than a human thumb no wider!

There's a stone amid the mountain
and amid the stone a hollow
which a drill has bored into it
and a bodkin pierced into it:
drive the pains down in the hollow
and the evil hurts conceal there
pack sharp agony into it
all our days of need press downwards
that by day they may be useless
and by day be ineffective."

So sang Väinämöinen to Kivutar, pain-daughter, and to Vammatar, the daughter of hurt; then he sang to Ukko himself, and the song and the nine sicknesses were over.

"So the people of Kalevala are well again, are they?" said Louhi. "And what about their animals—their horses and their cattle? I'll see what I can do to them now."

A few days after the healing of the sicknesses a great bear was seen in Kalevala, wandering about and viciously attacked anything that crossed its path. All the beasts of the land went in terror of their lives. Väinämöinen knew that such a huge bear could only have come from Louhi; he asked Ilmarinen to forge him a long spear, and he went out across the plains to hunt the bear.

"This is no hardship that Louhi has sent us," said Väinämöinen as he stalked through a forest, "for if I catch the bear we can have a feast."

Of course, a spear, however long and sharp it may be, is of little use without singing, just as ointments will heal only with the help of a charm; so, as he plodded along with his spear and a coil of rope, Väinämöinen sang. After the usual forest-songs to Tapio and his wife, Väinämöinen sang to the bear itself:

> "*Otsonen, my peerless darling*
> *honey handed one, sweet bruin!*
> *Lay your head upon the hummocks*
> *comfortably on the bed-rocks*
> *underneath the swaying pine trees*
> *underneath the whispering spruce trees.*
> *Otso, trample out your couch there*
> *honey handed one, turn around there*
> *as upon her nest the partridge*
> *as the goose when she is hatching!*"

The bear could not resist such superb singing, and Väinämöinen soon tracked it down and had it secure on the end of his rope. The best way to keep fresh meat fresh is to keep it alive, so instead of killing the bear immediately he dragged it back through the forest and across the plains to his home.

There was feasting indeed that night. Pans sizzled with the bear meat, songs rose into the dusk with the smoke from the fires. Väinämöinen sang the praises of Tapio and the forest matron, with whose help the bear had been caught; then he sang the praises of the bear, which was big enough to feed the whole of Kalevala. So wonderful were Väinämöinen's songs that night that even the moon and the sun, which during the summer nights sit low in the sky opposite each other, each waiting for the other to move first perhaps, both stepped down to earth so that they could listen without straining their ears.

Yes, that night the moon settled in a crooked birch tree in Kalevala, and the sun sat in the branches of a pine tree. At least, that is what folk say; and if the moon and the sun did not, how could Louhi have done what she did—in as little time as it takes to sing a middle-sized song?

Suddenly the land was plunged into darkness—total darkness in midsummer! Or was it midwinter now? Väinämöinen and the people of Kalevala stopped their merrymaking and groped their way gloomily homeward—only to find that all their fires had gone out, leaving their dwelling quite cheerless. The strange thing was that however hard they tried to rekindle their cold hearths, they could not raise so much as a spark in the whole puzzled land.

Meanwhile, far away to the north, an old woman, her bony shoulders shaking with wicked laughter, was carrying a flaming bundle into a mountain cave. It was Louhi, Mistress of the North. She had seen the moon and the sun step down out of the sky, and, while all eyes and ears were on Väinämöinen as he sang, she had come to Kalevala, grabbed the two globes of light from their perches and whisked them away to her storehouse in the Copper Mountain, taking the fires of Kalevala too for good measure!

"Hm, what's going on, then?" murmured a disgruntled Ukko in his high home beyond the clouds. He had noticed the all too sudden change from midsummer to midwinter, from heat and light to cold and darkness, and he was beginning to feel uneasy; someone was trying to do his job for him, someone was interfering! How could he organize the days and the seasons properly, if this sort of thing went on behind his back, that was what he wanted to know! Or perhaps it was the fault of the moon, the sun and the fire themselves; perhaps they were unhappy with the way he was running the world? Well, they had only to come to him and talk matters over, not go dashing off without his permission just because they felt like it! Where were they, anyway?

"Now, don't lose your temper," he told himself, and to show whoever might be watching that he was in a good mood, he put on his pale blue stockings with the heels darned in all colors, and loped around the sky, peering behind all the clouds as he went. Not a sign of the rascals! Or had the poor things been kidnapped? He would find them sooner or later—after all, he was Chief Spirit and he could deal with most problems. In the meantime, though, something must be done to replace them.

Ukko drew his sword, and swish! across the sky it went, giving out a shower of sparks like stars. With great care he picked one up, and cupping his windy hands around it he carried it to the maiden who looked after the air for him.

"Rock this spark and bring it up well," he told her, "and when it's big enough I'll make it into a new moon and a new sun."

The sky-maiden took the spark and laid it gently in a cradle of clouds. A little spark, all to herself! The maiden was delighted. She would show Ukko what a fine nurse she was, she would make him really proud of her, she thought. She seized the cradle and began rocking it with all her might. The whole sky creaked and groaned like a wooden house in a gale as she rocked the spark, to and fro, to and fro, to and . . . oh. She had rocked it so hard that it had fallen out of its cloud-cradle. To her horror she saw it tumble down, down through the dark sky, trailing a long streak of fire as it fell. It was as though the air had flung all its windows open.

"Ilmarinen, look!" cried Väinämöinen, jumping about as old men seldom do. "Come on, let's go and see where the fire has fallen. It may be a piece of the fire we've lost."

The two men ran off toward where the spark had fallen. They had not gone far when they came to a river, a very wide river because it was just about to pour itself into a lake. They must cross it if they were to go on. Neither of them felt much like swimming all that way in the dark, but what else could they do?

The answer, of course, was to build a boat; which they promptly did, and within minutes they were afloat.

"Who, or who are you?" came a soft, sighing voice from somewhere. The heroes looked about them, there was nobody to be seen.

"We are sailors for the time being. I am Väinämöinen, and this is my friend Ilmarinen. But who are you?"

As they listened to the sound of the lapping waves, they realized who it was.

"I," said the voice, "am the Water Mother, ageless Mother Nature, your mother. And where are you going, where?"

"We have lost the moon, the sun and the fire, O Mother. We have just seen a flame fall out of the sky, and we are going to see whether it is a piece of the fire that has vanished from our land."

"Oh, that fire!" sighed the Water Mother. "It has done so much damage, burning houses and scorching people wherever it has gone."

"Where is it now?" asked Väinämöinen.

"It roared its way through villages and forests, danced over marshes, and plunged into a lake, where it drove all the fish up on to the shores. The fish wept and panted as they lay homeless on the sand, until one brave little fish dived back into the water and swallowed it, in the hope that the fire would be quenched. But no, the fire raged inside the little fish, making it dart about in pain. Anyway, thanks to the little fish the lake had stopped boiling, and all the fish returned to their homes.

"Now," the Water Mother went on, a trout happened to see the little fish in distress. If I swallow the little fish, thought the trout, surely the fire will go out —and I shall get a meal into the bargain. So the trout swallowed the little fish. But the fire did not go out, and the trout swam around and around the lake in terrible pain. Then a pike happened to see the trout. If I swallow the trout, thought the pike, surely the fire will go out—and I shall get a meal into the bargain. So the pike leaped forward and swallowed the trout. But still the fire did not go out, and the pike scared all the other fish more than ever by dashing here and there, gulping as it had never gulped before.

"And that," said the Water Mother, "is where the fire is now—inside a little fish inside a trout inside a pike."

There was no time to waste. The heroes rowed to the lake, where they made a huge net. They let it down into the water, and dragged it to the shore bulging with all manner of fish. They sorted through their catch, and—ah! there was the pike which had swallowed the trout which had swallowed the little fish which had swallowed the fire.

They cut open the pike and found the trout; then they cut open the trout and found the little fish; then they cut open the little fish, and there was the fire. Väinämöinen was just working out the best way of taking it home, when the fire flared up in his face, and tore away over the water and through the forest on the opposite shore.

The two men jumped into their boat, crossed the lake, jumped out and chased the fire through the forest, till at length they caught up with it. Väinämöinen addressed it politely as it glowered and crackled at his feet.

"Good fire," he said, "this is no life, wandering about idle and homeless, for a creature as noble and as clever as you. Why not come home with us? You'll have a fine stone hearth to live in, and plenty of useful work to keep you happy."

The fire thought for a moment, and with a flicker decided that it was quite a good idea. It smoldered while Väinämöinen nimbly picked it up and put it in his tinder box, where it made friends immediately with a small piece of birch fungus.

Once again the homes of Kalevala were warm and the kettles were singing for joy in the hearths. But the land was still in darkness, with nothing to brighten the hours of night and no daylight at all. Crops were destroyed by frost, the breath of cattle rose like steam in the meadows, and birds died.

Thanks to the fire, however, Ilmarinen was able to continue his work. One day among the smoke and sparks he had a brilliant idea; he would forge a moon and a sun of iron! Eagerly he did so, and hopefully he hung his iron moon in the crooked birch tree, where the real moon had last been seen, and his iron sun he suspended in the branches of the pine tree, from which the real sun had vanished. Very impressive they looked, but of course they were only two lumps of iron, and the land was as dark as ever.

"It's about time we found out what's become of our moon and sun," said Väinämöinen when the people could bear the darkness no longer. "I wonder whether the sticks will tell us?"

He gathered some twigs of alder and arranged them in his hand. To anybody else, of course, there is nothing so dumb as a bundle of alder twigs, but to Väinämöinen they said a great deal.

"I must go to the North Land," he announced to the people, "and I promise you it won't be long now before

138

the moon and the sun are back in their places."

Väinämöinen set off, and after a weary journey he reached the Copper Mountain, where the moon and the sun were locked away; but since the stealing of the Sampo old Louhi had had stronger locks and bolts fixed on the mountain's door, and no amount of tugging, striking or even singing would move them.

When Väinämöinen was back in Kalevala he went straight to Ilmarinen.

"Ilmarinen," he said, "make me a spear with three points, a dozen hatchets and an enormous bunch of keys. I need them to rescue the moon and the sun."

As Ilmarinen was beating out the tools, he heard a rushing sound outside the smithy. He went to the window to see whether there was a wind blowing up; but no, a large, fierce looking hawk had settled beneath his window.

"Hullo, hawk," said Ilmarinen, just as though it were a man—or an old woman, "and what can I do for you?"

"O great Ilmarinen," screeched the hawk as graciously as it could, "you are indeed a most skillful craftsman!"

"So I should think," said Ilmarinen without batting an eyelid; "it was I who forged the dome of the sky, you know."

There was a pause in this strange conversation, then, "Tell me, O smith," said the hawk, "what are you working on today?"

"A ring," replied Ilmarinen darkly, "a big ring to fasten around old Louhi's neck, and chain her to a mountain."

Without so much as a good-day—which, besides, would have sounded foolish—the hawk disappeared. Ilmarinen shrugged his shoulders and went back to his grim task. He was thinking how light the sky outside had suddenly grown, when another bird came to his window. This time it was a soft, white dove.

"Hullo, dove," he said, "and what can I do for you?"

"I've news for you," cooed the dove, "the moon and the sun are back where they belong—look!" And the dove fluttered away to the North Land, where it too changed back into old Louhi. She had grown tired of the darkness as well, and of what use are the moon and the sun if they are locked inside a mountain? A peaceful life, she decided, was better after all.

Ilmarinen went to the door of his smithy and looked; yes, there were the moon and the sun, shining opposite each other in the midsummer sky for all they were worth. Ilmarinen forgot about neck rings, three-pointed spears, hatchets and bunches of keys, and ran all the way to his friend's house.

"Väinämöinen! Väinämöinen!" he laughed, slapping him on the back, "come out and see the moon! Come out and see the sun!"

Väinämöinen raised his old eyes to where Ilmarinen was pointing, and he sang with a full heart:

"Hail O moon for your pale shining
lovely now your face revealing
precious daylight freshly breaking
hail O sun for your bright rising!
Precious moon from rock delivered
lovely daylight from the mountain
risen like a golden cuckoo
risen like a dove of silver
high into your former dwelling
high into your ancient pathways.

Rise for ever in the morning
from this day henceforth for ever!
Greet us always with good mornings
fortunate, bring us good fortune
catch good catches for your fingers
happiness upon our fish hooks!

Go now on your way with greeting
on your pathway with our blessing
let your airy vault be lovely
come into your joy at evening!"

MIGHTY MUSIC

nce there was a girl called Marjatta, which means Little Berry. Marjatta lived with her father and mother, and as the years passed she grew into a lovely, kind and gentle young woman; but she was very shy.

Perhaps this was because she had to spend so much of her time alone in the hills, tending her father's sheep, instead of meeting the other girls and the young men in the village. Day after day she would sit among the grasses and the bright spring flowers, listening to the cuckoo and sighing, "How much longer must I stay alone in these hills, looking after sheep? One summer more, or five, or ten? Or . . . or is the time coming for me to leave home already?" she said, for she suddenly had a curious feeling that it was.

On her way home one evening she saw a bush crowded with small, dark red berries. She was thirsty after sitting in the sun, and the cranberries looked delicious. She plucked one and put it in her mouth, little berry, she thought, like Marjatta.

Time passed and Marjatta grew very quiet and wanted to be left alone. She has been spending too much time in the hills, thought her parents, and now she is growing fat and stupid, like the sheep she looks after.

One day she went to her mother and said, "Mother,

will you heat the bath house for me?" At that time the *sauna* had two uses; one, of course, was for having a steam bath; the other was for giving birth—its warm, damp atmosphere was ideal for bringing babies into the world. Marjatta's mother was just going to tell her to heat it for herself if she wanted a bath, when she noticed something about her daughter. Marjatta was not simply fat, there was a child under her heart waiting to be born!

"So you've found yourself a husband without consulting us!" said her mother indignantly.

"No, I haven't, Mother," said Marjatta. "There are no young men in the hills, there are only berries."

"What sort of nonsense is this?" her father joined in. "You've clearly married without our permission, and you must have your baby at your husband's house, not here!"

Marjatta was bewildered and a little frightened. Why were her parents so angry with her, especially since she had done nothing to displease them? And how, how was it that she was expecting a child?

"Only one thing I know," said Marjatta sadly as she left home, "my baby will be a great man one day— greater even than Väinämöinen!" And she dragged herself off to find a bath house in the village.

No room! No room! Wherever she went it was the same answer. In despair she wandered away into the forest beyond the village.

To her relief she soon found shelter, it was only a stable, but it was warm and there was plenty of hay. The horse whose home it was must have been surprised at such an unexpected visitor.

"Good horse," said Marjatta as she sank into the hay, "breathe over me. I'm so cold and tired."

While the horse snorted and blew its soothing clouds of sweet, warm breath over her, Marjatta gave birth to a beautiful baby boy.

How she cared for him, washing him in the horse's trough, feeding him, patting him on the back, laying him in her lap, dressing him and combing his tuft of hair! No, thought Marjatta, she was not lonely any more, now that she had a little son; nobody else mattered as long as he was content.

Then, suddenly, one day he disappeared. What could have happened to him? Marjatta wondered as she searched frantically. He was not in the stable. Who could have taken him? He was hardly big enough yet to go off on his own. Marjatta looked everywhere, under stones, behind trees, in the long grasses she looked, carefully sorting every leaf and blade; but he was nowhere to be seen.

That night, as she continued her search and was wondering where to look next, she saw a star high above her.

"Star, star," she called, "where is my little boy?"

"Even if I knew," the star replied rudely, "I shouldn't

tell you. Your boy is my master, and it's thanks to him I have to shine up here through the cold nights, when everyone else is tucked up in bed."

"Moon, moon," called Marjatta when she had looked still further, "where is my little boy?"

"Even if I knew," the moon replied just as unpleasantly, "I shouldn't tell you. Your boy is my master, and it's thanks to him I do nothing but night work, and have to sleep all day when everyone else is enjoying life."

All through the night Marjatta searched, until by dawn she was at her wits' end with worry.

"Sun, oh sun," she called when it was hardly light, "surely you've seen my little boy?"

"Your little boy?" repeated the sun, beaming. "He's my master, and I've so much to thank him for as I wake the world from darkness and sleep. Yes, I've seen him, he's sitting quite happily over there in a marsh." And the sun pointed a warm finger of light.

Overjoyed, Marjatta ran across the marsh, swept her son up into her arms and carried him back to the stable, singing at the top of her voice. How had he come to be in the marsh? This was another question to which there seemed to be no answer; and if the star, the moon and the sun called him their master, she mused as she put him to bed, there would probably be many more questions without answers.

One week, two weeks passed, and the baby grew strong and chubby.

"It's time you had a name, young scamp," said Marjatta one morning, as he lay looking up at her with wide blue eyes. "But what shall I call you? I'm sure you deserve a special name." Marjatta tried to think of a special name, but only ordinary, everyday names came into her head.

"I know," she said, "I'll find an old, wise man and ask him. He'll know more special names than I do." So she took her baby through the forest to find an old, wise man.

"Excuse me, can I help?" said a voice behind her. Marjatta turned around, and there, believe it or not, stood an old man.

"I am Virokannas," said the old man. "You seem to be looking for somebody."

"Well, yes, I am," replied Marjatta. Virok-annas, she thought, that means John the Namer. "I'm looking for somebody to name my baby, and since you are Virokannas, I wonder if you'd be kind enough to think of a name for him?"

"If you find somebody who will tell me all about him," said the old man, "then I will name him, for I can see that this is no ordinary child."

"This is where I can be of use," said a familiar voice. It was Väinämöinen; he was very old now, and looking rather frail. "This boy?" he said as the child blinked in his mother's arms, "I know all about him. Born of Marjatta—little berry, hm, I suggest you stick him back on the bush!"

146

Of course, Väinämöinen knew what the child was, and he was simply jealous. He had enjoyed leading the people of Kalevala down the years, and now this wretched boy was going to take over from him.

As for Marjatta, she had had enough surprises already; but now came the biggest surprise of all.

"That's not fair, you silly old man!" It was the baby speaking! "Nobody stuck you back on a bush, did they? And what would have happened to this land of ours if they had? Don't you see that you're too old to lead your people now? You've brought them up to be a nation, and now they need a king."

It was an awkward moment. Quickly Virokannas seized the child from Marjatta.

"You, child," he said, "I name King of this land, and Lord of all power." And giving him back to his proud mother, the old man hurried off.

Väinämöinen was still angry, but he knew his work was done. As he walked through the trees down to a lake where his boat was moored, he realized how glad he was after all that his beloved Kalevala had a king at last, for he was very tired.

> Then the aged Väinämöinen
> set out sailing on his journey
> sailing in his brass-trimmed vessel
> sailing in his boat of copper
> sailing to earth's higher places
> sailing to the lower heavens.

There he vanished with his vessel
weary with his boat passed over.
But his kantele *he left us*
and to Finland left sweet singing
to her people joy for ever
mighty music to her children.